D0395145

The Pages Between Us
In the Spotlight

Lindsey Leavitt
Robin Mellom

HARPER

An Imprint of HarperCollinsPublishers

Library of Congress Control Number: 2016949958
ISBN 978-0-06-237774-6 (trade bdg.)

Interior Design by Abby Dening
Doodle Artwork by Abby Dening
17 18 19 20 21   CG/LSCH   10 9 8 7 6 5 4 3 2 1
❖
First Edition

From Robin: For Lindsey (you know why)

From Lindsey: For Robin (you know why)

Dear Passerby:

That's great that you found this non-interesting
collection of nothing, but this isn't for you.
Please put the notebook back where you found it.

Thanks,
Management

Seriously. If you found a dirty sock, would you keep it? No. You would not. So leave this notebook alone. It is a dirty sock.*

*Ew.

Last chance.

Step away slowly.

There you go.

Whew. I think it's safe now. Piper, meet me on the
next page. →

Piper,

You. Me. This top secret notebook. Together again! Finally!!

It felt like winter break lasted forever, but in a mere nine hours, forty-three minutes, we will be walking through the doors of Kennedy Middle School, where every student will be sporting brand-new itchy sweaters. Yay! (I think.)

The plan will be the same—we'll drop off the notebook in our lockers and exchange it in the hallway between classes. Let's document every step of the way for fun. Or as my dad, the Coolest Anthropologist in California, would say, "For anthropology's sake!"

Our wise words could educate the little green aliens when they someday beam down here. (Or do aliens beam *up* here? Come on, scientists. We need answers!) Not that aliens should read this since we made it very clear this notebook is off-limits.

These are our secrets.

Our precious thoughts.

Our "only my best friend will understand" letters.

Perhaps we should have made it clear to the aliens . . . "Do not read even if you're not a human and from the future."

It's possible aliens-from-the-future will be very gossipy.

Also, the Martians could steal all our amazing double wedding ideas, and suddenly everyone will have six-foot-long banana splits at their reception, and our original idea won't be original anymore.

Stay on your own planet, please.

So here I am sitting on my bed staring at Blinkie as I wait for school to start. He's meowing a lot tonight. Maybe he's nervous for me.

Am I nervous? Hold on.

I just asked Blinkie. He blinked twice.

As we all know, my cat blinks once for YES, twice for NO.

And guess what! He's right—I'm *not* nervous. Which is practically headline news. You know how I get when I have to deal with change—it turns my stomach into a knot. The tricky kind of knot you have to learn for a Girl Scout badge. Usually going back to school puts me in Full Worried Mode.

What if it's too warm inside to wear this sweater and I, you know . . . sweat?

What if headbands suddenly went out of style over the holidays?

What if I'm assigned a report that has to be read out loud . . . in front of PEOPLE?

But that's the *old* me; even more specifically, it's December me. *January* me has decided to take charge of her life.

Be bold.

Be fearless.

No, I didn't read any self-help books over winter break. It's better than that!

Remember when I told you I started having lunch in Ms. Benson's office once a week? Well, it's supposed to be a friendly chat, but she's been using her guidance counselor skills on me. I can tell. My guess is once you get your counseling degree, you can't really turn it off, lunchtime or not.

Anyway, lately she's been giving me strategies to deal with anxiety. But I don't like calling it anxiety (because that word makes me . . . anxious). I call it Worry Wort Syndrome (WWS), which is a more accurate description of me. Or it was.

Ms. Benson told me all about this thing called "catastrophic thinking," which is figuring out the worst thing that could happen and then letting that thought bounce around in your head until you almost convince yourself that awful thing will definitely happen.

She says I'm supposed to question my thoughts like I'm some sort of detective getting to the facts. During our last meeting, we examined my catastrophic thinking about not giving my brother the perfect Christmas gift and how I assumed he'd be disappointed because it wasn't cool enough for his college dorm room and he'd get all moody and mean and our holiday would be ruined.

Catastrophic thinking.

So I cross-examined my thoughts and realized that wasn't the most likely outcome. She had me close my eyes and imagine the best thing that could happen. I imagined Jason loving his gift and then asking me to play a game of chess. (And yes, I imagined that I was wearing a super snazzy business suit for all this. My imagination is very classy.)

Guess what happened! Jason loved his Snoopy calendar and we played chess, but not just one game . . . four games! And we also went to the mall together without Mom, just the two of us having fun and eating waffle fries.

I was wrong to assume my winter break was going to be a disaster. It went amazingly well!

Ms. Benson was right when she said that life can be surprising sometimes—that things can actually turn out better than we ever imagined.

So!

That brings us to January.

It marks the beginning of the year, and I'm excited to get back to Chess Club and the animal shelter. January also means it's my favorite time of year . . . no, not the annual clearance sale at the Yarn Hut—that's *your* favorite time of the year.

For me, of course, it's time for Battle of the Books. My annual tradition! I get to talk to other readers about books. Study the story and characters. Answer reading comprehension questions at a competition. Can you spell H-E-A-V-E-N??

Sign-ups were in October, but I haven't heard much about it since. This explains why I'm so excited because tomorrow—tomorrow!—is the first meeting. It's during lunch, which makes it even more exciting . . . books and food. Who *wouldn't* want to go? I'm sure our librarian, Miss Nikki, has lots of plans to make this amazing. Oh, sheesh, I need to stop calling her Miss Nikki because that's what the kids called her when she worked in the elementary school. I know this because she sometimes volunteers at the public library and I see all the little kids crowd around her. "Miss Nikki! Miss Nikki!" They don't even have actual questions; the kids just like calling out her name. Like she's a rock star.

Now that she's here—in serious middle-school territory—we have to call her by her "proper" name: Miss del Rosario. Which I honestly love so much more. It rolls right off your tongue and into a bowl of luscious chocolate. Sophistication is what I'm going for here.

I'm not sure what will happen at this first meeting. I heard that our middle school has placed last in the competition for three years in a row. I hope we can turn that around since Miss del Rosario is here now. Being on a losing team is . . . well . . . my worst nightmare. But it'll be okay—I have lots of ideas about how we can get everyone to learn the information quickly. Maybe I'll email my ideas to Miss del Rosario.

Oh! Speaking of emails . . . (Note: this next paragraph has nothing to do with emails. It's all about Jackson Whittaker. But you knew that.)

I have some Jackson news. But I'm not even going to tell you about it yet. Getting panicky about conversations with boys is *so* last December. I'll tell you all about it in my next letter.

Cool as a cucumber—that's me.

So tell me everything that's been happening. Every detail! Let's start January off with a notebook celebration! Which means we should meet sometime soon out at the tide pools—our sacred spot. We'll do our best this time to not stand directly under any pelicans flying by.

Let's rock the rest of this sixth-grade year.

Januarily yours,

Olivia

As always, my five gratefuls:

1. This notebook
2. The brand-new sweater I'm wearing tomorrow (Embroidered daisies—total cuteness without, hopefully, any embarrassing sweat!)
3. Battle of the Books
4. Tide pools
5. This notebook (It's a repeat of #1, but it deserves this much admiration.)

Oh! And I've attached our family's Holiday Newsletter. Mom and Dad were so busy that they didn't get around to writing it so I offered to do it. Which is why it was sent out late this year. Also, I'm not sure if I'm doing "Holiday Newsletter!" correctly. Other people seem so cheerful. I just really like numbers and math.

All Mom had was this University of Georgia stationery. Bulldogs aren't super festive, but oh well.

THE WESTON FAMILY'S ANNUAL HOLIDAY NEWSLETTER

Greetings,

We hope you are having fun. And eating food. And asking your kids a bunch of questions. That's what the holidays are for, right?

Here is our year by the numbers:

31: number of weeks until the Georgia Bulldog football season starts

3: number of chess matches Olivia attended

1574: year of Dad's favorite civilization

6: number of parties Mom held for the University of Georgia football games

14: number of University of Georgia Rice Krispie Treats Olivia consumed

2: number of times Jason visited us from college

1: number of cats named Blinkie that still live with us

We wish you the best this coming year. Hopefully nothing bad happens to you.

The Westons

Hi, friends!

Merry Christmas! I love Christmas card season, because I finally get to put all my skills from the stationery store to good use. Also, I'm hardly ever on the social medias (or computer. I know! I'm awful with technology), so I miss out on updates from everyone. That's what I love about letters—they're a great way to reconnect. In fact, one of my New Year's resolutions is to write more letters. I probably won't, but a mom can dream. :)

We miss you all and hope you had a wonderful year. Here's an update on our little piece of the universe.

The Jorgensen Clan

RUBEN: Ruben is working hard as Mr. Brake. We are opening another shop in Thousand Oaks next year, so he's spent lots of time scouting and hiring. He's also the new Sunday school teacher at our church! Ruben went on an Alaskan fishing trip with college buddies in September . . . just for the halibut (his joke, not mine). He's also started to grow out a beard and I must say, even after twenty years of marriage, he is one handsome guy.

BROOKE: I'm still working part-time at Doodlebug stationery store. I love the store displays and interacting with customers . . . stocking isn't my favorite task. I'm also taking photography classes at Cal Poly, focusing on portraits. And of course, I'm escorting kids to their various activities and sometimes I even get a meal on the table. I love what I do.

LUKE (17): Luke took all-state for the second year in a row in volleyball. He's already looking into schools, and he's only a junior.

We spent three weeks last summer checking out different colleges—he has a favorite but I'm not allowed to say. He's also big into CrossFit. Still a very accomplished cellist. Grown three inches in one year!

TALIN (14): Oh boy, Talin has blossomed this last year. Such a beauty. She's also on the straight-A honor roll and growing as a pianist. She volunteers at the library and the food bank, where she feeds the homeless during the holidays. She's turning into such an accomplished, graceful girl.

PIPER (12): Piper is just . . . Piper! She loves playing with her brothers and helps me with babysitting. I won't even tell you the name of her favorite TV show, because I'm not totally sure she should be watching it. :)

FLYNN (3): Funniest kid. Star of his soccer team. Scores goals until they have to drag him off the field. Still carries blankie everywhere with him. Random women stop me in the store all the time so they can touch his curls. Starts art academy with Spencer this spring.

SPENCER (3): Spencer still loves eating vegetables. I could give him a piece of cake and he would ask for a bell pepper. He knows 178 words in Spanish. It started off with flash cards, but now he watches language videos and starts a Spanish class next summer. He is *muy inteligente*!

And that's us! Another year of fun and crazy. Wouldn't change this group of all-stars for anything.

Merry Christmas to you and yours!
THE JORGENSENS

Dearest, darlingest Olivia,

Why didn't I have you write *our* Christmas card too? I added it to the notebook. I didn't include the family photo because it's just so awful.

This is what you don't see in the family photo: Flynn throwing up three minutes after the picture was taken. Or Talin getting mad at Mom because of the matching plaid shirts. Or the photographer singing the jingle from Dad's Mr. Brake commercial.

What you also don't see is *me*. I'm blocked by Talin's head. Is this supposed to be a metaphor, Olivia? We learned about literary devices in reading. And I'm pretty sure that is a metaphor for my place in the family. Perhaps even my lonely place in the world. This is just like our family fridge.

There's an article from the newspaper when Luke got all-state. There's also a program from Talin's last performance. There are notes from teachers, pictures the twins drew, clips . . . but nothing like that for me. Yes, there are a few photos, but nothing broadcasting my extreme awesome.

That one line keeps echoing in my head. "Piper is just . . . Piper!"

It's like my mom couldn't think of anything else to say about me. All my siblings have these long lists of achievements and Mom makes it sound like I'm some lonely cat lady who watches soap operas all day. (Which, I should mention, is not a bad thing. The plotlines and characters in *Love and Deception* are preparing me for real-life situations. If someone ever goes into a sudden coma or takes on a fake identity, they'll all come running to me for answers.)

I have other things going on. She didn't mention the animal shelter, or LARPing, or knitting. I mean, I had this big birthday party with all these new friends just a few weeks ago. I totally proved that I'm able to make friends, even if my motivation was sort of tied into the Drama! Intrigue! and Scandal! of it all.

And what about my videos?! Guess who documents all of Talin's piano recitals and Luke's games? It's good old Piper-just-Piper with the camcorder I got two Christmases ago. Then I edit those videos so that they're not the most boring things on earth to watch. And when I'm babysitting, so the rest of my family can go out and do all these amazing things, I write and direct videos of my twin brothers. Which, yes, only have twelve views on YouTube, but I've been so focused on the creative side, I haven't done much marketing.

Whew. Okay. I'm not bothered by this. Well, not really. I'm just confused. Nothing I do is very refrigerator-brag-worthy. I don't know how to be more than "just" me. But I'll figure it out. And keep you posted.

Otherwise, Christmas was all:

CARAMEL ROLLS!
SNICKERDOODLES!
HOMEMADE
FUDGE!
STICKY FINGERS!

Oh, and I guess there was family time and presents and yuletide spirits in there, but I thought I would mention the important thing (FOOD) first. The scarves I knit everyone were a hit. You were right to choose the color of yarn that I thought fit their personality. Luke has worn his burgundy one every day of break, and I don't think it's to be nice. It's not like we live in the arctic, so I appreciate the gesture.

Our church class did this Favorite Things party where you bring five of the same item and leave with a basket of random goodies. Of course, my mom—the gift basket queen—was very jealous. I knit beanies, and Bethany almost got in a fight with Tessa over the green one. Which was so sweet! I've never made an accessory so desirable that people almost shed blood trying to get it.

Sorry I couldn't hang out this weekend. Friday I had to do back-to-school chores and babysit the twins. We made a video where I cooked all these weird food combos then recorded the twins eating them and grossing out. Spencer kept saying Spanish words like *"ay, caramba!"*

But it came out as "I kawumby!" Crazy cute.

So far, only nine views, but I could make those kids *stars*.

Here's what I really want to tell you about though. On Saturday, I babysat for Andrea. It's always weird to say "babysat" with Andrea, because we are sort of friends. And we . . . sort of play. Saturday night was My Little Pony night. Poor Pinkie Pie got in a fight with Fluttershy for stealing her boyfriend, but Fluttershy couldn't help it because she drank a truth serum from Buzz Lightyear (there aren't many boy My Little Ponies. Clearly a creative limitation).

The babysitting part was normal, but then Danny came

home with his parents. I guess his dad volunteers for a non-profit that donates water filters to developing countries, and Danny helps out so he went to a gala. His mom had on a ball gown and Danny wore a suit. A suit!

So then, they're standing there in all their fanciness, and after the awkward part where Mrs. Moss pays me money, Danny says, "You don't need to drive her. I'll walk Piper home."

Liv. What? WHAT?

I couldn't say no! Because things are still a little strange with Danny Moss. He used to be super rude to me every time I walked by his dumb lemonade stand. Then he asked me to set him up with Tessa. Then that little fight happened at LEGO Club and I accidentally gave him a bloody nose. Then he came to my birthday party. Voluntarily. Almost happily, I think. And now . . . he wants to walk me home? Olivia. If aliens actually do read our notebook someday, maybe they can explain the weirdness of Danny Moss.

Mr. Moss slapped Danny on the back and said, "That's my son. Yes, walk Piper home. Don't be out too late."

So ten minutes after Rainbow Dash almost lost her pony life in a tragic rock slide, I'm kicking a rock down the street while Danny Moss walks next to me. Whistling. He was *whistling*.

"Did you have fun playing with my sister?" he asked.

I shot him a look. "Don't make fun of me."

"I'm not." He held up his hands. "I think it's great that you play with her. You're a good babysitter. I usually make her watch skateboarding videos with me."

Skateboarding videos? Obviously Andrea doesn't want to watch stupid videos like that. Where's the drama?

"How was the gala thing?" I asked.

"Way cool." He smiled. He already got his braces off. The braces worked, if you're wondering. "They raised a lot of money. I like that kind of stuff."

I kicked at a rock again. "Good. I like when you're gone so your mom pays me money to watch your sister."

He laughed. "Yeah, it's not a bad business if you structure it right. If you get your referral source solid, I'm sure you can increase your hourly asking price. And then people will think you're better at childcare, just because you ask for more money. It's like when I'm selling lemonade. If I charge a dollar, people assume it's organic water or something and they drink it slowly."

"Um, thanks for the business tip?" Was that a business tip? I was so confused.

"I'm not going to give you all the Andrea babysitting business, though. It's too lucrative."

I didn't know what *lucrative* meant. "Fine, I'm not trying to steal your job."

"I didn't say you were."

"Okay. Whatever." I think we were kind of fighting all of a sudden. I don't know why it started. My Little Pony plotlines are much easier to figure out.

"Wait, it's not like that." He sighed. "I like to help my parents, but sometimes I feel like I'm just their personal assistant. That probably sounds dumb."

It didn't sound dumb. I almost told him about that "Piper is just Piper" line, but it's Danny. I can't say those kinds of things to anyone except you. Imagine if I told *Danny* that kind of stuff.

But do you notice what was happening, Olivia? Danny was telling me things. Being nice to me. And I'd already set him up with Tessa, so it wasn't about that, especially since they hate each other now.

So what WAS it about? I keep thinking about it. Do you think he's like Randall Menard in *Love and Deception*? Baiting me with lies and kindness only to double-cross me in the end? Or is he doing that business talk because he wants me to invest my babysitting money in his lemonade stand?

TRANSLATE. PLEASE.

And finally . . . I'm glad you are excited about school

starting again. Of course, that means progress reports come out in the next couple of weeks. I haven't been, um, totally focused on my grades. So I'm a teeny tiny bit worried. What color do you wear when you're worried again? Should I knit a worried-color beanie?

Love you, bestie,

Pipes

Grateful: Holiday treats, this strawberry lip gloss I got in my stocking, My Little Ponies and all their deep dark secrets, the scarves I'm going to make with the yarn I got for Christmas!, youyouyouyou

Piper,

Magenta. It's always my go-to color when I'm worried. But you don't need to worry about grades. Just keep up with the homework and that big essay for literature and never, *ever* use a red pen in Mr. Marsdale's class—he hates that.

This Danny thing needs more research. He would definitely be the Randall Menard type if he sometimes wore a fedora and scratched his chin all evil-like (I think Randall Menard does that? I've only watched five episodes with you and I have no idea how you keep it all straight). Anyway, maybe Danny's just being friendly? My parents always say that boys will start doing the nice thing once they "mature." Honestly, the thing you should be worried about is whether he thinks you're a friend or a friiiiiiiiieeeeeeeennnnd-with-a-winky-face. (I'm not sure what that means either. Ignore me.)

Okay, so this morning in homeroom, I was feeling very magenta. But I quickly started feeling turquoise, my go-to color for hopefulness.

Then magenta.

Then back to turquoise.

Let me explain.

The first ten minutes of homeroom—I will admit—were filled with utter weirdness. Since we'd all been away from each other for two weeks, it was almost like the first day of school when you walk around like a sleepy zombie not knowing how to engage in a conversation.

So there we were . . . all sitting in class, all wearing warm clothes, all wiping our eyes from tiredness, all not knowing what to say.

Just.

Weird.

That's when I thought of the best possible outcome in this moment, like Ms. Benson taught me. I imagined myself wearing a flowy blouse and skirt (again, my imagination . . . super classy), and carrying on a downright lovely conversation with that girl Felicity Armenta. And guess what! That's what happened. (Minus the imaginary classy outfit.)

I turned around to face Felicity and asked what she got for Christmas. We ended up having a nice conversation about rainbow-striped socks, which was conversationally awesome of me! I say this because other kids around us joined in and started talking to each other and it felt like Felicity and I broke the tension in the room. They instantly fell back into chatter like we'd all just seen each other yesterday.

But Mr. Kunkel rubbed his temples. "Quiet!" he said, like he'd suddenly come down with a migraine. Then he grabbed a stack of handouts. "Principal Dawn has made some changes to the rules. The halls have become chaotic and we need you to move in an orderly fashion when we change classes. Please read this and sign and date it at the bottom stating that you are aware of and agree with the new rules."

All this "signing" and "agreeing" and "being made aware of" suddenly worried me in a super magenta type of way.

The hallways are the one chance to talk to people we don't normally see.

And in case you don't know who I'm talking about, I'm talking about you. We use hallway time to exchange the notebook. And sometimes we sneak in a quick, "Hey, girl!"

I really really hope we don't lose those brief glimpses of each other. But after looking over this handout, what if I never have another human interaction via hallway ever again?

You guys got this handout in your homeroom, right? →

Kennedy Middle School

To: All Kennedy Middle School Families

RE: Hallway Traffic

Dear students and parents,

In an attempt to improve the traffic flow in the hallways, I am implementing a new Hallway Initiative. Starting today, all students are required to walk only two-by-two and no passing is allowed. That way, we will cut down on the number of injuries that have occurred from students opening their lockers and being knocked over by someone passing on the right. Our nurse's office has been far too busy lately.

Initiative? Sounds like a government program to fix highways or something.

For reals? What if I'm engaged in meaningf[ul] conversati[on] during a walk-n-talk with two people?! Oh, wait. I would only walk-talk with you.

But passing is so much fun!

Also, keep those elbows in. For everyone's safety.

↑ Elbow discrimination, I say.

Thank you,

Principal Dawn*

And possible dictator—or maybe Roman Emperor? Empress? That's more dramatic.

What good is school if all you focus on is your classes? There are interesting people out there to talk to! Probably!

Now, let's see . . . was there something else I was going to talk about?

taps chin for dramatic effect

Oh! Yes! It's news about a boy named Jackson Whittaker.

(Also known as: JACKSON WHITTAKER!!!!!)

Yesterday, I stopped by Boomers because Bethany told me a bunch of kids from Kennedy Middle School would be there playing putt-putt golf. (Sorry you were babysitting. Again. For the twelfth time in a week.)

So who happened to be at Boomers also? Jackson Whittaker.

(Also known as: JACKSON WHITTAKER!!!!!)

Sorry, got screamy.

There I was trying really hard to get my neon-pink ball to roll gently into the hole of a giant fake windmill when he stepped up next to me and started talking.

That's right. HE stepped up to ME and started using WORDS close to my FACE. My heart did a backflip/herkie jump combo.

Aaaaand it sticks the landing!

I could hardly breathe.

Luckily, he started the conversation. "What's your score?"

Heart triple flip.

"Um, five." I had no idea. Bethany was supposed to be writing things down on that pad of paper with the little stumpy pencil, but she kept getting distracted by the people around us. She cheered them all on, because as you know . . . she has a cheering disorder. She takes full advantage of any situation where it's appropriate to throw her hands in the air and say, "Woohoo!"

"Start in the corner on this hole." Jackson leaned over and placed my neon-pink ball in a different spot, then motioned for me to begin putt-putting. (Man, I love that word. Putt-putting really should get used in everyday language far more than it does.)

Plunk!

He was right. I *did* need to start in the corner. Hole in one, baby!

So then this really crazy thing happened where he asked a question, I answered. I asked a question, he answered. Like it was Verbal Tennis.

Some words that were included in the conversation:

Golf ball

Windmill

AstroTurf

Northwest winds

Humidity

Macaroni and cheese

Elbow numbness

Things that are fancy-schmancy

Algebra homework

Soooooo . . . add all that up and we talked for almost fifteen minutes. FIFTEEN MINUTES. And I didn't even die.

I think that since my mind was highly involved in my putt-putting, it was too busy to overthink things and get worried and stumble over my words.

It was awesome, actually. But now I'm not sure what to do or say when I see him in school. Like, is he now going to expect all our conversations to last fifteen minutes and go amazingly well?! I DON'T KNOW IF I CAN RE-CREATE THIS MAGIC!!!

Sorry. Got screamy. Again.

The school does not allow golf clubs. I checked the website. So now I need to find activities to occupy my brain when he is nearby. This could get complicated.

Now I'm going to put all my energy into hoping lunch gets here soon. I can't wait to meet with Miss del Rosario and find out how many people are signed up for Battle of the Books.

I'm sure Bethany got the word out to all her Bethanites. Are you sure I can't force you into signing up? It's just ten books you have to read. It's fun!

Battle of the Books on the Brain,

Olivia

Gratefuls:

1. Starting a conversation with Felicity Armenta
2. My daisy sweater that did not cause me to sweat
3. The fourteen candy canes still left over from the holidays
4. The Lazy Cats calendar my brother gave me for Christmas
5. All the awesome ideas Miss del Rosario has for Battle of the Books (Technically that's a *pre*-grateful since we haven't had the first meeting yet, but Ms. Benson tells me to put positive thoughts into the universe and sometimes they happen!)

Olivia,

Do you know what a principal's job is? Like, when someone applies for the job, there must be a description. Something like . . .

WANTED: MIDDLE SCHOOL PRINCIPAL
REQUIREMENTS: *Must have gone to school for a long time and taught for a long time and know how to deal with children*
TASKS: *Being in charge of discipline and schedules and stuff that requires signatures*
PAY: *Not enough*
BONUS: *You should be really, really into order and conduct. Especially conduct. Be prepared to discuss your views on hallways. Hallways are dangerous. Be prepared!*

They're calling it an *initiative*? I don't even know what an initiative is. What I *do* know is, if you treat kids like cattle, they are going to moo back at some point. If they take away our exchange moments, I will moo so hard.

MOOOOOOOOO!

I got new stickers from the stationery store!!!

I'm knitting a scarf right now. It's magenta—the worry color, right? It might turn into a body scarf, actually. Because my first day back was super fun. (Sarcasm! But you already knew that.)

I ate lunch with the Bethanites—Bethany, Tessa, and Eve. I can call them that, now that I'm sort of one of them.

"Isn't back-to-school fun?" Bethany asked as I slid my tray onto the table. The rest of the girls packed their lunches. Oh, by the way, I guess exotic cheese, crackers, and sliced vegetables are the new "it" cafeteria food. I went for the salad bar and poured ranch on everything, including my shirt.

"If by fun you mean F. U. N.—Freaky, Ugly, and NOT fun, then yes. Super fun," I said.

Tessa leaned in. "But seriously. It is way too hot to wear this leather jacket my mom got me. Even if it is amaze!"

"Someday everyone will remember that we live in California and not Connecticut and we should stop pretending winter is an actual thing here," I said, then remembered my manners. "But, I mean, yeah. That jacket is amazing." Tessa called it "amaze" because she doesn't like using any word over two syllables, but I feel we should slow down our lives and allow *multiple* syllables. Call me old-fashioned.

"Did you get anything good for Christmas?" Tessa asked me.

"A case for my camcorder. And a new battery," I said.

Tessa seemed confused by this, so I added, "And lip gloss."

Bethany flipped her hair. "We already talked about Christmas. Let's talk school. I'm so so excited about midterms!"

Eve laughed. Bethany shot her a look.

"Oh, you're serious?" Eve asked.

You know, Eve might be my new second-best friend (after you). Because I totally agreed with her. Enjoyment of midterms = crazy laughter.

"Do you think our teachers sit around during holiday break, rubbing their hands together and plotting their next assignment?" I asked. "Like they miss giving out assignments so much that they add up three weeks' worth of F. U. N. into one day?"

Bethany spread some brie cheese on a water cracker and frowned. "No, I think they enjoy their hard-earned vacation. Besides, teachers make such meager salaries, I'm sure they're in this profession because they love what they do . . ."

I popped a garbanzo bean into my mouth and zoned her out. Bethany and Tessa are in super-smart-kid classes. I couldn't start to tell them how I really felt about school.

Here's a page torn out from my school planner of upcoming assignments . . .

	Math	English	French
Monday	Mrs. Dudley wants us to add fractions. And the bottom numbers are different. Bottom numbers that are different make my head spin.		Brainstorm Edible Structure ideas
Tuesday	Fractions HWK due	Can't I just write the word "Hatchet" over and over again? I have no idea how to write reporty things about booky things. Ugh.	We're supposed to make a famous Frenc structure out of an edible object? Gumm Bear Eiffel Tower? Is this supposed to be educational? Non.
Wednesday		A book report on that book HATCHET.	

The thing about school is . . . I try. I really do. I don't 100 percent *care* about everything we are learning all the time, but I know it's important to learn stuff so I can write business letters someday or balance a checkbook or open my own snickerdoodle delivery company. Although nobody has probably balanced a checkbook since 1995, but I would never tell the life skills teacher that. But snickerdoodle delivery? I'd almost go to a tutor willingly if I thought I could do that for a job.

I wish we could be graded on the things I'm naturally good at. Like knitting. And babysitting. And spilling ranch dressing on my new Christmas sweater. And being your friend. And making videos.

Anyway, that's cool about Battle of the Books. Let's not make this like Chess Club, okay? We already know I'm not doing it. Reading *one* book is enough of a battle for me. Actually, I don't think I've ever actually done it. Read a book all the way through. At least one that wasn't for school. Don't tell anyone. I kind of skim when I get bored, which is usually after the first chapter. I would much much rather watch the story happen. But that's just me.

Remember in fifth grade when we did the door decorating contest? Each class had to wrap the door in paper and find some cute way to advertise books? Our teacher stuck twenty titles up there and you READ EVERY BOOK ON THAT DOOR. That was bonkers. You are so amazing. I feel like I'm smarter just because I know you.

Anyway, I'm jumping out of my bad mood, because it's a brown place to be and brown isn't a very fun color (more like a F. U. N. color). But magenta is a fun color. You're a winter color, so you should wear lots of magenta. Bethany Livingston taught me that.

Non-brownly yours,

Piper

Grateful: Some brown things . . . like brownies and gravy, the end of the school day, sarcasm, youyouyouyou

KENNEDY MIDDLE SCHOOLERS!

Book it over to the library and sign up for this year's

Battle of the Books!

Who can do it? YOU! It's not too late!
You just need to read these ten awesome books . . .

6ᵀᴴ GRADE BOOK LIST

- ★ *Charlotte's Web*, by E.B. White
- ★ *A Crooked Kind of Perfect*, by Linda Urban
- ★ *Little House on the Prairie*, by Laura Ingalls Wilder
- ★ *Holes*, by Louis Sachar
- ★ *The Hunger Games,* by Suzanne Collins
- ★ *The Seventh Wish,* by Kate Messner
- ★ *The Mysterious Benedict Society,* by Trenton Lee Stewart
- ★ *Out of My Mind,* by Sharon Draper
- ★ *Cinder,* by Marissa Meyer
- ★ *Old Yeller,* by Fred Gipson

Battle of the Books is a trivia challenge.
You will participate in games and fun activities to prepare you
for the mock battle. One team from each school will go to the
district competition! We compete with all the middle schools
in our district. It's an entire day off from school!
And yes, there will be pizza! Join today!

Piper,

That flyer makes me bouncy. This may come as no shock, but I've already read the required books. Some of them twice.

I got the list last fall and started right away. I really, really want to get on the school team that goes to the district battle. In elementary school, I went to district every year, but now it's different. Middle school different.

The books are harder.

Longer.

Plottier.

Can I get a "Woohoo!"

So today was surprisingly surprising.

Follow along:

1. I arrived for the meeting early. No surprise there.
2. Miss del Rosario was busy putting up posters on the walls of the library.
3. I held the pushpins for her while she teetered on a ladder.
4. Naturally, I took the opportunity to tell her all about

my previous experience with Battle of the Books and how I was team captain in fifth grade. And fourth grade. And third grade. And how disappointed I was in second grade to find out that it wasn't offered to students that young and I even wrote a letter to the editor at our local paper and they actually printed it and I was sort of famous for almost a day and a half.

5. When I was done explaining my résumé, I asked, "Can I see the list of people who are coming to the meeting?"

6. Her face suddenly turned white. "Actually . . . I need to talk to you about that."

7. FYI: when an adult says, "I need to talk to you," it's never something you want to hear. No adult has ever said those words and then followed it up with a surprise! Trip! To Disneyland! So I fiddled with my sleeve, nervous about the non-Disney-related sentence she was about to say.

8. She grabbed a clipboard from the counter and started to hand it over.

9. But then she didn't hand it over.

10. Instead she yanked it back and clutched it tightly. "Before I show this to you, please understand that I am new this year and the program has previously

been a little . . . oh, how do I say this . . . put on the back burner because of testing, so a lot of changes need to be made—"

11. "Changes, yeah, sure." I reached out. "Can I see the names?"

12. "—since I'm a new librarian here I've had to work very hard to make Battle of the Books a priority—"

13. "You worked hard. Got it. Can I see—"

14. Then she just blurted it all out at once. "Kennedy Middle School has come in last place at the district battle for the past three years, which means the level of interest in the competition is, well . . ."

15. This is where she paused to finally shove the clipboard in my hands.

16. It was a list.

17. A list of names.

18. Names of people who signed up for Battle of the Books.

19. I looked it over and realized why Miss del Rosario's face had suddenly turned marshmallow-colored.

I should have said puffy-cloud-colored; that would've been cuter. My apologies for this weirdness.

20. Guess whose names were on there.

21. Mine.

22. Bethany Livingston's.

23. That's it.

24. There wasn't actually someone with the name "That's it." There were two names. TWO? How could this be? I'm sure Bethany spread the word about it—she has a blog that is perfect for this sort of news-spreading. So seeing only two people had signed up made no sense. I'd been using my positive-thinking skills, so why was Battle of the Books now threatening to turn my stomach into a Girl Scout knot?

25. Miss del Rosario shook her head. "No one seems interested in joining. We don't even have enough people to make a team. Administration told me the deadline to send in our teams is next month. We must have two teams to participate in the school battle."

26. I quickly did the math in my head. Each team has one captain and three members, plus an alternate. To make two teams, we would need to get eight more people signed up. By next month.

27. I explained all that to Miss del Rosario. She said, "This won't be easy. I'm so sorry it happened this way. I've been giving out those flyers and making displays

of all the books, but . . ." Here she sighed—deeply. "This is all so heartbreaking. I was a student here at Kennedy and I participated in the battle. I loved it."

28. I smiled. Big and wide. Our own librarian was a student here and participated in the Battle of the Books years ago. How amazing is that?

29. "What's up, ladies?! Let's get this battle started!" It was Bethany, clutching a bundle of balloons. "Where should I put these?"

30. Miss del Rosario pointed to the table she had decorated with a tablecloth and flowers and napkins in the shapes of books. BOOK-SHAPED NAPKINS! (Which are just rectangles, but let me have a moment here.)

31. Bethany looked left, then right. She lifted a brow. "Um . . . am I early? Why are we the only ones in here?"

32. Then we heard the door slowly creak open. It was Ian Speloni. He was on my team last year in elementary school. He constantly shuffles and wears his hoodie over his head and spends all his time in the library looking through aviation books. Library Lurker . . . that's what everyone called him. Probably still do. But the guy reads—almost all the time. So at that point I was happy to have him lurking near our meeting.

33. Without saying a word, he grabbed a handful of pret-
    zels and slumped into a chair.

34. "But I told everyone I know about it." Bethany put
    her hands on her hips. "I told everyone on my bus.
    My church friends. Everyone within a ten-locker
    radius of mine. It's even up on the Events section on
    my blog." She paused. Waited for an explanation. But
    all I could do was shrug. Bethany flipped her hair
    over her shoulder. "Ooooooo-kay then. How are we
    going to beat Laguna Middle School with only three
    of us? I heard from Kyra Thapa, who heard from her
    neighbor's older sister, that Laguna is our rival—the
    team to beat." She stepped closer to Miss del Rosario.
    "I don't like losing competitions. Like ever."

35. It was at that moment that I thought Miss del Rosario
    would pat her on the shoulder and be reassuring and
    come up with some epic plan to recruit warm bodies.
    Instead, this happened: "I'm worried we won't find
    enough students to join. I made so many flyers—and
    colorful ones too. I even put it in the newsletter." She
    dropped her head. "I've failed you all."

36. Sheesh, Miss del Rosario. Talk about catastrophic
    thinking.

37. Bethany sighed, then skipped back over to the snack

table to scarf down some pretzels. She was probably hungry from only eating fancy cheese and crackers earlier.

38. Library Lurker strummed his fingers on a table.

39. This. Was. Awful.

40. Then my voice—without my permission—suddenly got squeaky and desperate and I sort of fell into a bowl of catastrophic thinking too. "So what are we going to do? Battle of the Books is really important to me. Reading is my favorite hobby next to chess. Maybe I like it even more than chess. Books are better than movies, better than video games, better than . . ."

41. Wow, I was really going off the rails here. ". . . and they're better than *most of the internet*. What if we can't find—"

42. And then it happened. The grinning. Miss del Rosario would not stop grinning.

43. She placed her hands on my shoulders. "Olivia. You. YOU could help make this a huge success!"

44. Um. What was happening?

45. "When someone loves books as much as you do, it's contagious. You should share your excitement for the competition, Olivia!"

46. "Contagious? How do I spread the word?" I asked. "Sneeze?"

47. "Kids listen to their peers. So you could get the word out." She turned to Bethany and Library Lurker. "Will you two help out?" LL pulled his hoodie tighter and didn't answer. "I'll blog about it," Bethany said. "But my schedule is packed." So Miss del Rosario turned to face me, like I was her only hope—her literary Obi Wan. "Olivia, if we don't have enough students volunteer to make two teams, I'll have to tell Principal Dawn that the battle will be canceled."

48. Whoa. Two things happened in that moment. One: I freaked out at the thought of the school *not* doing the competition. Two: I freaked out at the thought of her saying, "Get the word out."

49. Basically, lots of freaking out was taking place.

50. Did "get the word out" mean I'd have to say something? In front of a group? Out loud? From my *mouth*?

51. Get it together, Olivia. Deep breaths. Positive thinking. All that stuff.

52. Number 51 is all the stuff I was saying in my head.

53. Miss del Rosario clasped her hands together, looking

very excited. "You could make posters asking students to come to our next informational meeting. You could be our guest speaker. It will make them want to join!"

54. I fainted.

55. Not really.

56. But I wanted to.

57. No, wait.

58. That was *old* me.

59. The previous five sentences probably didn't deserve their own separate numbers.

60. But whatever.

61. "I could put a mention about your posters on my blog," Bethany said. "I get, like, fifty-four page views a day."

62. Except Bethany has already talked about Battle of the Books on her blog. I think if her people were going to join, they would have already.

63. Miss del Rosario must have thought the same thing. "Don't worry. I can up the wow factor by using my Marni puppet."

64. Piper. Do you know who Marni puppet is? So . . . before coming to Kennedy Middle School, Miss del Rosario was a librarian at Eisenhower Elementary

School. Have I ever mentioned Miss del Rosario and I chat a lot? She always comes to the public library reading events so we go waaaaaay back. She's one of my personal heroes.

65. Okay, okay, I realize this story is already taking up over sixty numbers, but bear with me here.

66. Anyway. She would use this sock puppet named Marni to get the kids all excited about books. Marni has a raspy voice and a love of rhyme. Second graders adore Marni.

67. But middle schoolers?

68. They would not adore Marni.

69. Had she lost her mind?!

70. I needed to bring her back to earth.

71. "How about you keep Marni in her box," I said.

72. Bethany crinkled her nose. "Seriously."

73. "I'll figure out something to say and . . . and bring a bunch of donuts!" I said. "The warm ones from Krispy Kreme!" I don't know where that idea came from, but sometimes when you're backed in a corner with only the option of listening to Marni puppet or coming up with a different idea . . . well, you come up with a different idea.

74. Warm donuts.

75. "It could work," Bethany said.

76. Which brings me to the color turquoise. Hopefulness.

77. I'm going to pull on my best turquoise sweater and hope that a poster for an informational meeting that includes Krispy Kreme donuts will be enough for us to form a team and make all this catastrophic thinking go away.

78. But if this poster-and-donuts idea doesn't work, then could you come up with an amazing idea?

79. "Yes, Olivia! Absolutely!" said you. Hopefully.

80. I didn't want to end on an odd number. Done now.

Girl who will never let Marni puppet come out of her box,

Olivia

Grateful: Well, I already made this letter all about lists, but I'm on a roll so let's do this.

1. Miss del Rosario's enthusiasm

2. Miss del Rosario trying to figure out a way to save the program

3. Miss del Rosario being worried about breaking the news to me that it could get canceled

4. Miss del Rosario's attachment to Marni puppet even though I hope she never pulls out Marni puppet

5. Miss del Rosario

Piper,

Me again. Sorry I didn't have time to drop this off in between classes. The reason is due to what I will call: THE POSTER-MAKING DISASTER OF THREE MINUTES AGO.

In art class, the teacher let me create Battle of the Books posters since it's educational and the librarian had technically "assigned" me this project. So I spent the entire fifty-two minutes adding glitter, puffy paint, decorative ribbons!

But at the end of class, I stepped out into the busy hallway and started to tape it onto the wall. That's when someone tapped my shoulder. "Sorry, Olivia. You can't post that."

I whirled around. It was Principal Dawn. In person!

"But I'm trying to get the word out about Battle of the Books."

She shook her head. "No posters—it's now added to the Hallway Initiative. We can't have posters falling off walls and causing a scene. I'm sure you can find another way to get the word out. Talking to people face-to-face is the best way." She then calmly took my poster and rolled it up. Glitter trailed behind her as Principal Dawn marched away with my beautiful, beautiful poster.

Which brings me to this: Principal Dawn said to talk to people. Specifically, their *faces*.

But I can't imagine myself walking up to strangers and suddenly being delightful. It sounds like the definition of the Worst Activity Ever.

So I don't know how I'm going to get the word out. With Bethany being fabulously busy all the time and Library Lurker tightening his hoodie all the time . . . we are stuck.

I need a magic button to fix this.

Hopeless, posterless, and magic buttonless,

Olivia

Liv,

I'm sure your poster had a lot of very carefully applied glitter involved, as well as origami and block letters. You may have even scented it in some way, which makes you a genius.

Posters are banned now? What?! Like they might ruin our childhood with all their dangerous behavior! That Hallway Initiative . . . aarrgh. It keeps growing by the minute.

But I have a solution for you! I, Piper Jorgensen, am your magic button. Let me tell you how I came up with this solution. It may even be better than donuts. Plus, your mom would have to stand in line for hours since Krispy Kreme gets mobbed every time the neon "Hot donuts!" sign turns on, and no one wants to wait that long.

In response to your last letter in list form, I will now explain your solution in list form.

1.   It was just your average day in the Jorgensen home.
2.   Talin had honor society and Luke had volleyball and Spencer had Spanish lessons and Mom had to do a shift at Doodlebug (apparently post-Christmas

inventory swap is very hectic in a stationery store).

3. Sometimes I still can't believe there is a whole store dedicated to paper.

4. So my dad had to leave his job at Mr. Brake to help with carpool.

5. You would think a man who owns a company called Mr. Brake would have a nice car. I'm sure at one point it was a nice car.

6. Probably back when Harrison Ford was the cutest man alive. (He's the guy who plays Indiana Jones in the old movies. Now it's evil grandpas or presidents.)

7. Anyway, we'd done all the sibling drop-offs and were headed home.

8. Since the heat didn't work in the car, Flynn and I were huddling in the back, fighting over his blanket, when my dad says, "I could use a hot chocolate. Who else wants one?"

9. Which is such a no-duh question. Sometimes adults ask total no-duh questions.

10. So we went to 7-Eleven. And I showed my dad the sad truth that he'd been drinking hot chocolate wrong his whole life. The trick is to add a good dairy creamer. I prefer Almond Joy. He liked Irish Cream. But that's okay.

11. Flynn got a Slurpee and spilled some on his shirt. But I told Dad this would likely happen, so we got him Piña Colada, which is white, and we felt pretty smart in that moment.

12. Then we were back in the car, which suddenly felt much warmer. Dad put on Creedence Clearwater Revival, which is this band from a million years ago, and we were singing loud, and wow. They're pretty good for being prehistoric.

13. It was such a *moment*.

14. One of those good ones you don't ever want to forget.

15. Then Dad smiled at me in the rearview mirror and asked, "So how's school going?"

16. And it's like the record scratched. Even though it was a radio, not a record. And he'd already turned down the music.

17. I didn't want to ruin this perfect little moment. In a family with five kids, there are a million family moments, but not many just-you-and-another-person moments.

18. Plus the twins. But they were playing some dinosaur/robot game at that point.

19. So I said the first thing that popped into my head: "It's great. Olivia is doing Battle of the Books."

20. I couldn't think of anything to say about me, so I said something about you. I should have mentioned LARP.

21. But I'm not sure my parents are totally on board with LARP yet. Like they never remember what LARP is. They'll say "Oh, is that when you dress up as a comic book character again?"

22. "No," I'll say. "That's cosplay. LARP is Live Action Role Play. You have a set world, and you can create your character within that world."

23. And then they'll say something like, "Oh, that's nice," or, "Mmmm-hmmm." Which are not answers of the highly interested. Which is why I mentioned your cool thing instead.

24. So then Dad says, "Battle of the Books? Is that where you read a bunch of books then have a trivia challenge about it?"

25. "Yeah." See! The details of *this* activity he remembers.

26. "Talin did Battle of the Books. That's so cool you're doing that, bug."

27. Notice I never said I was doing it, Olivia! But how lame would it be if I said, "Oh, I'm not doing it. My super cool friend is. I'm actually very stressed about

all these midyear assignments, so I just brought up my friend's awesomeness instead."

28. So then I said the second thing that popped into my head. Which was this:

29. "Yeah. It's pretty cool. I'm part of the publicity team. We want to make this the biggest year ever."

30. sdkfhsaifhaslifhlasihflaishfliahsflhsjflkhsdlgkjlds

31. WHY DID I SAY THAT?

32. I'll tell you why I said that. Because that line from the Christmas card popped into my head. You know . . .

33. "Piper is just Piper!"

34. And part of being Piper is making videos.

35. Which is a way you could publicize reading. Technically.

36. But I didn't say "video" to my dad. I said "publicize." I wasn't specific in case he thought a video was a bad idea . . . he's usually supportive, but what if he wasn't?

37. What if he said something like, "Well, reading is way more important than directing movies. Get it together."

38. He wouldn't say that last part. But he might *think* it.

39. And actually, my parents aren't always supportive about all the videos. If there was a hobby hierachy (I don't know how to spell that word), Talin and

Luke's activities would be way, way up on the Ladder of Important Things. My videos would be down in the dirt.

40. My parents have never said this *out loud*, but they have *shown* me how they feel many times.

41. Like did I ever tell you about the time that I had a bunch of my important videos on my memory card? Dad wanted to film Luke's volleyball practice so Luke could watch himself and figure out why his timing was off on blocking. Welp, Dad erased the whole card just to make room for Luke's practice. Not even a game, a practice. Hours and hours of my time—swoop! Gone. I hadn't even backed up the footage yet.

42. I think about this every time we're at another game or recital. On the hobby heriachy (did I spell it right this time?), my stuff is wipeable. My siblings' stuff is recordable.

My parents ———→

43. My point is, sometimes it's hard for me to tell my parents what I'm really thinking/feeling/experiencing. I don't want them to erase one of the things that show I'm MORE than Piper-just-Piper.

44. "Publicize?" Dad turned around in his seat and grinned. "So you're promoting literacy *and* reading the books? Good for you, Pipes."

45. Which is, I guess, half true. Or I could make half of it true.

46. Then I gulped down the rest of the hot chocolate. And the twins started to fight. And the moment was over after it barely started.

47. So.

48. Um.

49. I know BoB is totally your jam.

50. And I would never want to step on your toes.

51. But look at it this way. You need help getting the word out. And I need help having something to talk about when people, namely my parents, ask what I like to do.

52. So what if I made a video? Like, for serious.

53. I do *my* thing so that *your* thing can have enough people join it so it can actually *be* a thing.

54. I won't join the team and read the books or anything

because that would be like scratching nails on a chalkboard while pouring gas on old, smelly tennis balls. Something unlikable is what I was going for there.

55. Miss del Rosario can show the video in her library classes and it would be way way better than puppets.

56. No offense.

57. I can get Bethany to star in it! No, wait. She's probably too busy with clubs and blogging. I could use Felicity Armenta instead. That girl's a talker, as you know. I could set up a green screen in my garage while my parents are at work.

58. I'll also need to figure out how to make an animal look like it's flying, since that's totally in style right now.

59. And maybe add cartoons. There's a program that can turn you into a cartoon.

60. I'm so excited about this, Olivia. Seriously, I'll just make the video and then you can see what you think. If the donut idea works, great. But this can be an extra push and great for my future IMDB page.

61. And once I have an IMDB page, I'll show my parents and explain everything. But not until I have something that would boost me up higher on the family

hobby heirachy. (That word is tough!)

62. I already worked up a possible script. I couldn't help myself. :)

The Middlest Child That Ever Middled,

Piper

Grateful: VIDEO WRITING! VIDEO CASTING! VIDEO FILMING! VIDEO EDITING! VIDEO VIDEOING!

PROPOSED SCRIPT

FADE IN: *A helicopter is flying over the streets of New York. The helicopter pilot spots something on the ground. (He's played by Jude Mink, heartthrob star of* Love and Deception.) *He lands the helicopter and jumps out. In front of him is the beautiful Jane Suarez. (Also a star from* Love and Deception, *until her character was tragically killed in a paragliding vs. seagull incident, so I'm sure she could use the work.)*

HELICOPTER PILOT
PLAYED BY JUDE MINK
You. I've been looking for you!

FANCY LADY
PLAYED BY JANE SUAREZ
Me? Adorably fancy me?

PILOT *(Confused)*
No. Her! *(He points to Felicity—that girl in my LARP Club. She's standing just behind Fancy Lady munching on some snickerdoodles while reading a book. On a New York street corner! She is FABULOUS.)*

FELICITY

Me-ppfftt? *(Her mouth is full of cookie and it's hard to understand. I really hope Felicity is pro-cookie.)*

PILOT

You're reading *Pride and Prejudice*, by Jane Austen. It's my favorite book. I MUST know what you think of it. No, wait . . . the WORLD must know, fair maiden!

FELICITY

Uh. Okay. *(Wipes crumbs off her chin)*
The pilot leads Felicity into Rockefeller Center, where the Today *show is filmed. They find a stage and he asks a reporter to interview Felicity. (But it's not a stage on the* Today *show, Liv. It's actually my garage! Awesome, right?!)*

REPORTER WHO HAS NOW STRANGELY TURNED INTO JANE SUAREZ

(Our budget will be limited so I need to use actors in multiple roles. Super-famous directors do that. I think.)
Tell the world, Felicity. Look into that camera and tell the people of this planet exactly what you think of *Pride and Prejudice*. Everyone must know.

FELICITY

It's a great story. It teaches you a lot about how to get respect. And stand up for yourself. Probably. *(Is this right? Or is it about being a real person? Or finding true*

love? Death? Revenge? Redemption! Ohh . . . pride?
What if they had called the book Prejudice and Pride?
I find that catchier.)

REPORTER WHO IS STILL
STRANGELY JANE SUAREZ
Fabulous. And why do you read books? Why aren't
you currently playing Minecraft and eating Bugles? Or
listening to well-written pop music?

FELICITY
(The camera closes in. There are now stacks and
stacks of books behind her. Note: we need to find about
seven thousand books. Could you get on that? Or
maybe we Photoshop them in. Whatever. I just need it
to be dramatic.)
Because my parents are very strict on my electronics
usage, I have no choice but to read boring old books.
(Is this true? I don't know, maybe explain here why you
care about all this reading mumbo jumbo.)

*(Then end it with some dancing kittens
during this portion.)*

*(Again, could you get on this? Maybe borrow
a few baskets of kittens from somewhere.)*

**PILOT WHO IS NOW PLAYED BY
SPORTS STAR DEREK LANDERS**
(The director decided she wanted some celebrity diversity.)
(Derek Landers grabs Felicity's hand.)
We must go! The creepers are after you!
*(We need a villain, right? An ending with a
big chase scene will up our commercial appeal.)*

FELICITY
Let's book!
*(Again, Auto-Tuned because this will make her famous.
Or at least respected by my twin brothers.)*

*(Felicity jumps into the helicopter just before the big
explosion that blows up a good portion of Manhattan.
Then a huge Godzilla-size creeper from Minecraft tries
to destroy Brooklyn, but everyone is saved when the Hulk
rushes in with his baskets full of kittens and they scare
the creepers off with their adorableness. The Hulk is such
a softy. Who knew?)*

Whatcha think? Write back on my script.

END SCENE We can do this! (If I figure out all these computer
graphics and find some trained kittens.)

Piper,

Wow. Let me take a moment here.

Breathe, Olivia.

At first, your ideas made my stomach turn. So different. So out there. But I'm running out of time. And you might just be right—this could be my magic button to save the battle.

I can't believe I'm saying this but . . . let's give it a try! I knew you'd come to the rescue. Though it's a bit . . . hmm . . . what's the word . . . ambitious? My suggestions are below.

Honestly, your video idea came at the right time. This afternoon in Chess Club, I attempted to take Principal Dawn's advice and talk to someone face to face. There was one person I knew would listen to me: my partner, Ellie.

I leaned over the chessboard and whispered, "Hey, do you want to join Battle of the Books?"

"Check."

Oops, she was in a great position to take me down. I moved around a pawn and got out of that predicament. "Anyway. Books? We have a battle? Wanna join?"

"But I have homework. And clubs. And basketball."

"I know, I just thought—"

"You've been busy a lot lately. Sometimes you're reading during lunch instead of hanging out with me." She wouldn't look me in the eye.

"Sorry. It's battle preparation." Yes, I'm still rereading the books. My motto is: you can't be overprepared! But then again, all this preparing is taking up a lot of time.

She bit at her lip. "Then could you be sure to find me at lunch when you're not battling?"

I felt bad that we haven't hung out at lunch very much lately. "Sorry. Of course I'll come find you."

"Checkmate."

And that was that. She won and I lost out on convincing a friend to join the battle.

So . . . you don't have to join Battle of the Books. I get it—it's not your thing. Video-making IS your thing.

But I can't help but wonder why you felt you couldn't tell your dad that? Just because your dad reused a memory card or your sister's head is blocking you in the Christmas card doesn't mean you aren't a part of the family. Remember how I used to feel that way about Jason? That my parents only seemed concerned about him, but then I realized when I talked to them—*really* talked to them—about the stuff that's important to me . . . they did a miraculous thing: they understood. Weird, I know. But now I talk to my dad about Chess Club all the time and we even played four games together over the weekend.

Ms. Benson is teaching me how to take more control of my life. I'm supposed to ask for what I want and tell them why. She says people are more willing to do something for you if you explain why it's important. It's like the way you explained to your mother that this would be our Positivity Notebook, and BAM! She bought it for you and it wasn't even on sale.

So I told my dad I wanted to play chess with him because I wanted to learn and get better. I also told him it gets pretty lonely upstairs with only Blinkie. Since their bedroom is on the first floor, it sometimes feels like I'm some strange guest living in the upstairs apartment. But not anymore now that I'm following Ms. Benson's techniques.

I especially love this one poster above her desk. It says:

We cannot control the wind, but we can direct the sail.

Awesome, right? Make things go in the direction you want! This being-a-happy-person thing is really growing on me.

Anyway, after we laughed through our fourth game of

chess, Dad said he'd take me and Mom to Chevy's so we could order nachos and Mom could watch the UGA football game on the big screen over our shoulders.

Hooray for helpful posters!

So I know you always worry that you don't have a thing and you just babysit the twins, but my guess is your parents *don't* feel that way. Because you do have a thing. Lots of things. Next time, tell your dad about the videos, knitting . . . whatever you're into. I'm pretty sure they don't have a Hobby Hierarchy. Parents love their kids differently, not in some order of best to least.

Wow, listen to me sounding all glass-half-full and stuff. I could start my own talk show! Scratch that. Being on-screen in front of people would give me heart attack. Or make my head explode from embarrassment. Is that possible? I would look it up on YouTube but I'm afraid of seeing gross things I shouldn't be seeing. Can you imagine all the "related videos"? Ick.

But I will add . . . if you should happen to stumble and fall into a pile of approved books and you're stuck under something heavy and have nothing to do while you're waiting for the ambulance . . . you could read. And you could join my team. It would be fun for us to do something together.

If that's you under there, call me, okay?!

Let's talk about this more when we're volunteering at the pet shelter. Hopefully this week is "yard play!" and not "cage cleaning!"

Feeling peppy about pet shelter time,

Olivia

Gratefuls:

1. You and your magic button idea . . . it might just be magic!

2. That I got enough guts to ask someone face-to-face about joining the battle . . . even though I failed. Aren't there some good quotes out there about failure? My history teacher always talks about Thomas Edison being super okay with failing. And Edison turned out pretty well.

3. That Dad ordered double sour cream on our nachos at Chevy's

4. That Mom looked the other way when we ordered the double sour cream, but instead talked about us all watching *Gone with the Wind* together over the weekend. She says we'll understand her Southern roots more if we watch it. I should hope so—it's like seventeen hours long.

5. Your script!!

Speaking of script . . . on to my notes! →

PROPOSED SCRIPT

(I doubt Miss del Rosario has the budget for celebrities—she can't even get the school to turn on all the lights in the library.)

FADE IN: *A helicopter is flying over the streets of New York. The helicopter pilot spots something on the ground. (He's played by Jude Mink, heartthrob star of* Love and Deception.*) He lands the helicopter and jumps out. In front of him is the beautiful Jane Suarez. (Also a star from* Love and Deception, *until her character was tragically killed in a paragliding vs. seagull incident, so I'm sure she could use the work.)* Couldn't she do gum commercials? Surely she could find something better than a school-related promotional video. But what do I know about Hollywood?

HELICOPTER PILOT PLAYED BY JUDE MINK
You. I've been looking for you!

See above concerning celebrities and budgets. Bethany was in a couch newspaper ad once. Like you didn't know that. She talks about it ALL the time. Should we use her instead? I know she said she didn't have time to help out, but if you use the word "camera," she'll drop everything, I'm positive.

FANCY LADY PLAYED BY JANE SUAREZ
Me? Adorably fancy me?

PILOT (*Confused*)
No. Her! (*He points to Felicity—that girl in my LARP Club. She's standing just behind Fancy Lady munching on some snickerdoodles while reading a book. On a New York street corner! She is FABULOUS.*)

Does this mean you'll have your mom make snickerdoodles to use as a prop? If so . . . I SAY YES!

FELICITY

Me-ppfftt? *(Her mouth is full of cookie and it's hard to
understand. I really hope Felicity is pro-cookie.)*

PILOT

(Did this suddenly turn into a Grimm fairy tale?)

You're reading *Pride and Prejudice,* by Jane Austen. It's
my favorite book. I MUST know what you think of it.
No, wait . . . the WORLD must know, fair maiden!

FELICITY

*(Yes. We'll have to clean it up a little though.
No offense. I just don't think your brother's
volleyball stuff will be
the best backdrop.)*

Uh. Okay. *(Wipes crumbs off her chin)*
*The pilot leads Felicity into Rockefeller Center, where
the* Today *show is filmed. They find a stage and he asks a
reporter to interview Felicity. (But it's not a stage on the*
Today *show, Liv. It's actually my garage! Awesome, right?!)*

*(Not the famous directors—they use all the top-paid actors and
stomp around
all day complaining their
coffee isn't hot enough.
I think.)*

**REPORTER WHO HAS NOW STRANGELY
TURNED INTO JANE SUAREZ**

*(Our budget will be limited so I need to use actors in
multiple roles. Super-famous directors do that. I think.)*
Tell the world, Felicity. Look into that camera and tell the
people of this planet exactly what you think of *Pride and
Prejudice.* Everyone must know.

*(Jane Suarez-Turned-Reporter
is a little unbelievable. And let's have her tone
it down. "Her" meaning "Bethany" because of the
budget and all.)*

FELICITY

It's a great story. It teaches you a lot about how to get
respect. And stand up for yourself. Probably. *(Is this
right? Or is it about being a real person? Or finding true*

love? Death? Revenge? Redemption! Ohh . . . pride?
What if they had called the book Prejudice and Pride.
I find that catchier.) Jane Austen just rolled in her grave.

REPORTER WHO IS STILL
STRANGELY JANE SUAREZ 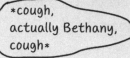 *cough, actually Bethany, cough*

Fabulous. And why do you read books? Why aren't
you currently playing Minecraft and eating Bugles? Or
listening to well-written pop music?

FELICITY

(The camera closes in. There are now stacks and
stacks of books behind her. Note: we need to find about
seven thousand books. Could you get on that? Or
maybe we Photoshop them in. Whatever. I just need it
to be dramatic.)

Because my parents are very strict on my electronics
usage, I have no choice but to read boring old books.
(Is this true? I don't know, maybe explain here why you
care about all this reading mumbo jumbo.)

NO!!! This is . . . this is the opposite of promoting literacy.
Instead I would have Felicity say: Books take you to another
world. You can learn about different ways of thinking. Learn
about love. And friendship. And humor—oh, man do I love a book
with humor. Books do that for me—they make life . . . better.
More than any movie or video game could. So tell Felicity to say
all that. She can call me if she needs help with deciding which
words to emphasize.

*(Then end it with some dancing kittens
during this portion.)*

> I will bring Blinkie. Best I can do.

*(Again, could you get on this? Maybe borrow
a few baskets of kittens from somewhere.)* ←

PILOT WHO IS NOW PLAYED BY
SPORTS STAR DEREK LANDERS

(The director decided she wanted some celebrity diversity.)
(Derek Landers grabs Felicity's hand.)
We must go! The creepers are after you!
*(We need a villain, right? An ending with a
big chase scene will up our commercial appeal.)* ←

> We don't need this to
> be Transformer cool.
> Just regular cool.

FELICITY
Let's book! ↙

> Uh, the fact that your toddler brothers will love
> this might be telling you something.

*(Again, Auto-Tuned because this will make her famous. Or
at least respected by my twin brothers.)*

*(Felicity jumps into the helicopter just before the big
explosion that blows up a good portion of Manhattan.
Then a huge Godzilla-size creeper from Minecraft tries
to destroy Brooklyn, but everyone is saved when the Hulk
rushes in with his baskets full of kittens and they scare
the creepers off with their adorableness. The Hulk is such
a softy. Who knew?)*

Whatcha think? Write back on my script.

END SCENE We can do this! (If I figure out all these computer
graphics and find some trained kittens.)

Piper . . . maybe we should think a teensy bit . . . smaller?

Olivia, Girl Who Loves the Books,

So I wish you could have come? For the filming? Even if it was a school night and your ~~overprotective~~ loving parents decided they didn't want you out after dark? Because the video didn't really turn out? And I don't know why I'm using question marks? But I can't stop?

You were right. I thought a little too big. I should have had production make some, er . . . budget cuts.

Someday if I actually become a famous director/ screenwriter/soap star, some cheerful E! reporter will interview me about my "start." I'll smile and look away from the camera, like I'm looking into the past. Then I'll share this hilarious story and laugh about how far I've come.

I'm just going to go ahead and make a word web of this "start" so you can see the highlights and major players in large bubbles. The bubbles soften things, I promise.

TRN OVR ⟶

THE BEACH: the tide pools were covered because it was high tide today so we had to go to Pismo. Everybody watched us film and then came over and asked, "So whatcha filming?" Filming on location can be so difficult!

There were a lot of pelicans out today. You remember what happens when there are a lot of pelicans. (Answer: poop.)

LOCATION

PIPER'S FIRST PAID GIG
(You don't have to pay me. I'm just saying this is different than the videos I make with the twins when I'm babysitting. Those are soooo dorky, I can't count them as my start!)

HELICOPTER: I actually got some good footage of Spencer's remote-controlled helicopter soaring across the water. Then it ran out of battery and plummeted into the ocean. So now I have to get him a new one, and the thing costs forty bucks!!

PROPS

THE HULK: I used Flynn's Hulk doll for the final HIGH STAKES! scene. We were all sorta giggly at that point and kept throwing the Hulk at each other like he had the cooties. Hulk cooties are a serious thing now.

BLINKIE: I put her in a basket on the beach and filmed her meowing. Best shot of the day. Think I'll use it in something else.

BETHANY LIVINGSTON: Grrr, I wish I could have Jane Suarez instead. Because Bethany kept giving me "ideas" to improve my artistic vision. Which basically meant if I told her to stand in one place she would say, "Oh, sorry, my good side is over here." Let's be honest. Bethany is pretty flawless—all her sides are good. Except the diva side, which I saw way too much of. And you were right—I said the word "camera" and suddenly she was at my doorstep.

ACTORS!

FELICITY ARMENTA: So Felicity apparently doesn't like cookies, so we had to do crackers instead for the cookie/cracker spitting part, and it just wasn't as funny. She really likes to e-nun-cee-ate things too, and sometimes it took her so long to say a word. Also, she totally flirted with Danny.

DANNY MOSS: Oh yeah, so obviously I couldn't get Jude Mink, even though I did reach out to his people/post on his Facebook fan page. So Danny saw the cast and camera crew leaving my house and asked what was going on. Felicity said we needed a male lead, he hopped on his skateboard and followed us over, and then he just kind of took over the role. He kept upstaging people with his straight teeth. It was annoying. Also, he told Bethany and Felicity they should unionize. What does that even mean? All I know is he made me pay him ten bucks!

Anyway, the whole thing is a hot mess, and I don't think it matters how much editing I do, this project really can't be saved. You'll be fine without the video. All you need is seven kids. How hard can that be? I'll find another way to prove myself to my family. Maybe I'll knit a scarf that can wrap around the entire equater (is that how you spell equater?).

And I already know you're going to ask me to join Battle of the Books. Love you but . . . no. Maybe pay Danny twenty bucks to join. That guy is always looking for a business opportunity.

Peace,

PIPE-A-RAMA

Domo arigato, Bethanites!

IT'S A NEW YEAR! Didn't last year go by super, super fast? We are now almost halfway through sixth grade, which practically makes us seventh graders. Which makes us ... well, I guess just getting older. Though some of you are getting cuter. You know who you are :)

Time sure does fly when you're having fun, and I had so much F-U-N over break. (Not F. U. N., which my friend Piper says is Freaky, Ugly, and Not fun. Aren't acronyms fu ... I mean, neat?)

My grandma Carol got me these amethyst earrings that are love love lovely. As readers of this blog know, amethyst is my birthstone and purple is my third-favorite color (although second-favorite color to wear), so I have been rocking them ever since.

Get it? Rocking it? Amethyst is a rock? Well,
actually, I guess it's a precious stone. But
"preciousing" is not a cute pun. And I know puns!

Which leads me to . . . Buzz Thursday! Here you'll find
all the buzz happening at Kennedy Middle School.
I mean, the buzz that *matters*. To me.

WHAT IS HOT

AMETHYST! (Obviously.)

Viral videos! (More specifically: kittens who play
patty-cake. Kittens who ride Roombas. Kittens in
baskets!)

All the new sweaters people are wearing—you guys
are impressive this year!

Progress reports: we get them next week. My dad
gives me a new accessory for every A. Claire's, here
I come!

SHOUT-OUTS

★ Awww, Tessa and Troy are going out! And you
  know it's love because it's been three weeks now

and they haven't had one fight. They don't see each other that much because Troy is technically not allowed to have a girlfriend yet (shhh), but absence just makes the heart grow fonder.

★ Jordan Goldberg: I know this sounds sort of cheesy, like something my grandma Carol would say, but this guy has the voice of an angel! He rocked his solo in the nativity performance over break. Good job singing, Jordan! You should totally try out for one of those TV singing competitions. I would vote for you! Twice, if they let us text our votes!

Oh, by the way, I think the Hallway Initiative will make it so people don't have to put their LIVES in danger anymore when they walk around school. But this morning Principal Dawn issued an update to the initiative and now we're not allowed to hang posters in the hallways because *apparently* Mira Watts tripped over a student council poster that had fallen to the ground and she did a somersault and got a split lip and needed stitches and somehow some mashed potatoes were on the floor. That last part is possibly just gossip, and as we all know, Bethanites . . . do not listen to gossip! But the no-more-posters thing is real. I just haven't confirmed the somersault and the mashed potatoes from a second source.

CELEBRITY GOSSIP

You know how Cameron Diaz is an environmentalist and trying to save California from this drought? I read an article that said people flush the toilet too much and it's, like, killing oceans. So Cameron Diaz doesn't flush when she pees! This is a direct quote: "If it's yellow, let it mellow. If it's brown, flush it down."

You guys.

WE NEED RAIN. I am not going to "let it mellow," thanks.

PERSONAL! UPDATE!

So I was invited over to Piper Jorgensen's house last night to help with a video. Making videos is my superpower since I was hired once to play the role of Ice

Cream Taster #3 in a Baskin Robbins commercial. I don't like to brag, but it was a great line to add to my résumé and I'm certain I'm on my way to breaking into the business. (People in "the business" say stuff like that all the time. They also "take" meetings, they don't "have" them. It's all so glamorous.)

Anyway! We were doing a promotional video for Battle of the Books because . . . hold up. I haven't told you guys the bad news yet.

There are only three people signed up for the competition. Me, of course, Ian Speloni, and Olivia, which makes sense because those two always have a book in their hands. But if we don't find seven more people, the battle will be canceled. I simply can't live without this competition! Participating in the battle is fantastic exposure for me and I honestly love all the books on the list.

So you *must* watch the video Piper made of us. The lighting was spectacular and I went to the salon for a blow-out, so I was completely camera-ready. I kept giving Piper my suggestions about my artistic vision and she kept shaking her head, probably because she was so baffled at how experienced and knowledgeable I am. Which is why I explained that I have a good side and to only shoot me from the left.

In case you didn't know, we ALL have good sides.

Which sounds super deep, but I'm actually just talking about the side of your face that looks fantastic. It really helps up the production quality when you shoot from the correct angle.

Join me in the battle, guys!!!

COMMENTS:

Danahuffhuff: I was there when Mira tripped over that student council poster. It was gnarly! Super stressful for me. I'm going to Cupcake Corner to help settle my nerves. Not so sure about this Battle thingy . . . read books? For fun? For reals?

DjTyler: That fall wasn't JUST from a student council poster. It also involved Troy Addelson's

foot and those two being all, "Whuuut?" and
then all of us being like, "Whoooooaaa." Just
a regular hall brawl. No reason for Dictator
Dawn to start up a Hall Program or whatever.
(Promise the principal doesn't read this!)

Bethanyblogs: I heard the Mira commotion but I
didn't witness it personally, so I'm going to take the
high road here and leave it up to the authorities.
And don't worry, Tyler . . . I always monitor my stats
and no one from school administration has checked
out my blog. Gossip away! (Er, not gossip. Simply tell
the truth. In an interesting way!) Later, Bethanites!!

Liv,

So I just saw you at the animal shelter. And you looked pretty today. Fantastic. Very glowy and sweet and healthy and . . .

Okay, I'll stop buttering you up. Look, I kept trying to bring this up tonight, but since it was Cage Cleaning Night, you had to stay focused on not breathing too much/keeping your dinner in your stomach. I had this idea after I read *Bethany's Business*. (Yes, I read every post now. She's my friend, but also she actually is pretty right about most things. Don't tell her I said that. Ever.)

Anyway, pretty, lovely, nice friend. As I said, the video shoot was a disaster. I've had a couple of days to go over the footage and . . . yep. Still a disaster. I just called Felicity, Bethany, and Danny to break the news to them. These are their responses . . .

BETHANY: Well, that's a bummer, Piper! I thought it went really well and I love your artistic vision. But to be honest, what I really care about is making sure Battle of the Books happens. So maybe you can use your super-creative brain to come up with another promotional idea instead? I sure hope so.

FELICITY: Hey, it happens. I'm just glad I got to meet that Danny. What. A. Cuuuue Tee. Maybe I'll come over to your house sometime so I can "accidentally" run into him. Also? You still owe me more of those organic crackers as payment.

DANNY: Whatever. I'm still keeping my ten bucks. The video was a weak advertising ploy. How would you even maximize exposure from it? Hey, I was looking at the list of books though. I've read a lot of those books. *Holes* is my favorite, have you read it? (Spoiler: no.)

So! Everyone is on board, or rather off board, with that project. But I don't think making a video was the problem really. I think the script I wrote was just . . . it was all wrong. I kept reading over it to figure out what was missing. And then I reread your script notes.

Your line about books not being wordy, but beautiful and "make the world make sense" . . . it made me realize something.

Even if I could get Jane Suarez and Jude Mink on board with the project, I still don't think I would use them. They don't have that special something. That passion. That knowledge. Basically, they are not . . .

And YOU! are what this video was missing! Your calm and thoughtfulness and beauty and grace. If I tried to say the things that need to be said, I would laugh.

So I'm working on a new script. I'll keep a few of my favorite parts/shots from the previous video. It will save us money and time. Good directors are always talking about money and time.

This video will be much more heartfelt and honest (I hope). This will reach into the hearts and minds of those seven Kennedy Middle School readers you are trying to find.

And you will triumph! As YouTube as my witness, VICTORY IS OURS!

Your humble director,

Piper

Grateful: Creative epiphanys (I can't spell that word!), Bethany still being cool even when she's super Bethany-y, the fact that I do office stuff at the shelter and not cage cleaning, tortilla chips, eyelash wishes

Piper,

By "you" did you mean "me"? I would look behind me to see
if you're actually talking to someone else, but that's not how
letter-writing works so I'm pretty sure you're saying *I* should
star in your video. Is that what you're saying?

Hold on, be right back . . .

Okay, I'm back. Had to do some nervous pacing outside
the cafeteria doors to take all this in. The problem is that I
actually do have lots to say about reading. Plenty. Tons. But,
Piper . . . I'm not the type to be a *star*. You know this.

I realize Ms. Benson has helped me be all: Take Control of
Your Life! Think Positive Thoughts! But being in the spotlight
isn't something I'd actually, you know . . . seek out.

Remember in fourth grade when we did a play production of
The Wizard of Oz and you played the part of the Cowardly Lion
(Lioness) and I played the part of Props Manager? I stood in the
wings so no one could see me and handed the actors their props
at just the right moment. I loved it. Being part of something big

like that and feeling needed but not being the *star*, was the best. I was quietly helpful. It's my favorite way to be.

Oh! In news related to the words "helpful" and "quiet," the weirdest thing happened in the hall this morning.

I was rolling up a poster Library Lurker had made for Battle of the Books. He doesn't talk much, so it was nice to see him try to help out by making a poster for us. Too bad he didn't realize the Hallway Initiative is growing in power like a hurricane. The poster—allegedly—fell to the floor and caused Desiree Winebrenner to slip and bonk her knee.

I realize the hallways can be chaotic, but changing school policy because of a "knee bonking" sounds, well . . . bonkers.

Back to the weird thing.

"Need some help?" It was Jordan. Goldberg. Jordan Goldberg.

I didn't need help. "Sure," I said.

He grabbed one end of the poster and helped me roll it up. He read the words as they disappeared, and then looked up at me. "I've read a lot of the books. I could probably join the team. Do you want me to?"

A huge smile filled my face. "Of course."

"'Sup, Jordan?" Jackson joined us and high-fived him. He looked over at me and flashed a semi-smile. Not a full one, but close. "What are you guys doing?" he asked.

"Rolling up this poster—it's a dangerous weapon," Jordan explained. "These things could cause serious knee damage."

I laughed.

Jackson didn't.

Then I kept my eyes on the poster and I rolled it tighter and tighter. Quietly I said, "It was for Battle of the Books." For some reason, I felt stupid for talking about it with Jackson. What if he thought it was completely uncool? I mean, he's the guy who makes amazing structures in LEGO Club. And he's the lead scorer on the basketball team. Does he even read for pleasure? And if he doesn't, will this be a big deal later in life when we're married and we have a heated debate about whether our child should win a Nobel Peace Prize or play quarterback for the Dallas Cowboys? I'm sure these are the things adults argue about.

It's possible I'm getting ahead of myself.

"Are you joining?" Jackson asked Jordan.

Jordan looked at me. Jackson looked at me. I looked at the wall.

What was going on?

Were they wanting my *opinion*?

Jordan stuffed his hands in his pockets. "Yeah. I'm gonna join."

"Maybe I will too," Jackson said.

Are you keeping count, Piper? Two. Two guys agreed to join the team in the span of four seconds. And not just ANY two guys. Jordan and Jackson . . . the two guys that make me feel . . . I don't know. Nervous? Confused? Full of butterflies?

All of the above?

But you know what? It also felt great. I'm not sure if they were joining because of me or because they actually like reading, but it wasn't all that important to me. I had managed to get two new team members and my toes were wiggling with excitement. Who says posters aren't great advertising?

Two down, five more to go!

So, maybe my brain has turned to Jell-O (and my heart! And my knees! Oh, hello there, Jell-O pinkies!), but I think I will do your video. What if I was able to encourage more people? It might be worth putting myself out there despite the danger of me dying-due-to-spotlight. If poster-rolling got this much of a response, imagine what a video can do.

But let's keep this low-key though, okay? I know how you get with your ideas . . . they start small and then tumble down Imagination Boulevard, rolling and gathering speed, and next thing we know, you're skydiving with a GoPro camera strapped to your helmet while wearing a Wonder Woman costume.

This is a joke,
NOT a suggestion.

Look, maybe—just *maybe*—we could share it with a few people in homeroom or I could take it to Chess Club. But let's stay away from YouTube. That place is really great for cats who chase their tails, but not so good for a girl who gets hives when more than three people look in her direction.

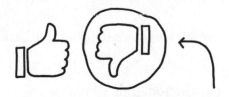

This is directly linked to my self-esteem.

I know that's two doodles in a row, but did I mention that Jackson is joining Battle of the Books? The thought of Jackson joining makes me automatically doodle.

Okay, I'm getting all the doodling under control.

So. I don't think we'll need Blinkie for this video since we're probably going for a more deep, cool indie vibe. I'll bring a sophisticated scarf instead.

This is new territory for me, Piper. But strangely, I feel like something amazing is about to happen. You know how some people say their elbow tingles when rain is about to come? My grandpa always says that. Well, I'm sort of feeling like that . . . my whole head is tingling.

This could be good.

Or.

You know . . .

Bad.

For now, I'm sticking with the good. I like that side of life.

Tonight, tonight, tonightly yours,

Olivia

NEW SCRIPT INVOLVING HEART!
HUMOR!
AND HEFTY EDITING SKILLS!

(Star Wars introduction . . .)
(The words get smaller and smaller as they scroll up the screen while space music plays.)

In a galaxy far, far away there were readers,
known to the aliens as "middle school students."
The act of reading seemed ridiculous.
So the opposition formed an alliance
with a galaxy of video game players
to thwart their plans of extreme literacy.
And this was their only response . . .

(Cut to Olivia wearing Princess Leia ear buns saying, "Help me, Obi-Wan Kenobi. Reading is my only hope!")

END SCENE

CUT TO a prairie
(Olivia is dressed in prairie-wear, eating a bowl of oatmeal.)

(Drops spoon in the wheat field. Or maybe a cornfield? Probably our soccer field. Gotta stick to the budget.)

LAURA INGALLS WILDER (played by Olivia)
The battle . . . the battle has begun!
(Runs into the house.)
(Inside the house, the dog is lying on the floor.)

LAURA INGALLS WILDER
Old Yeller! The battle has begun!
(Old Yeller runs away barking; he enters the forest and spots Katniss.)

OLD YELLER (played by my neighbor's Labrador, Duke)
Bark! Bark-bark-bark!
(Caption translates his barking: The battle! The battle has begun! I'm also hungry!)

KATNISS (played by Olivia, who is holding a bow and arrow and her hair is nicely braided)
I have to tell Gale. Or maybe Peeta. Or . . . I can't choose.
(Scrawls a note out on a paper. Shoots an arrow through it off into the distance.)

(Arrow and note land in a dirt hole in the desert)

STANLEY YELNATS (Olivia, wearing a dirty orange jumpsuit)
(Leans on a shovel and squints into the hot sun. Reads note out loud.)
The battle has begun?

FOREMAN (Danny) (if available and in a nice mood)
(Yelling) Keep digging for books!
(Stanley looks around, then climbs out of hole. Runs over to an outhouse. Opens outhouse door to find . . .)

SPIDER-MAN/CHARLOTTE from CHARLOTTE'S WEB
That's right, Kennedy Middle School! The battle has begun!

(Director's note: Look, Olivia, I know you don't want to wear Luke's old Spider-Man Halloween costume. But there are budget restraints. As in we have no money to go buy an actual spider costume. So this is how you "improvise" from the script.)

OLIVIA (in a Spider-Man costume)
I'm not saying the line. This is stupid.

DIRECTOR
(From behind camera. Can't believe how unprofessional her actor is acting.)
It's one line. Just say the one line and then we can eat snickerdoodles.

OLIVIA
Wearing a Spider-Man costume is not the same as being an *actual* spider from *Charlotte's Web*. E. B. White would not like this.

PIPER
What do we care what E. B. White thinks? Who is that?

OLIVIA
The author of the book we are not portraying. (sighs) I
need to talk to my agent.

PIPER (in a spidery voice from behind the camera)
The battle has begun!

OLIVIA
Were you trying to sound like me?

FADE TO BLACK
(FADE IN *with Olivia sitting on the couch, wearing*
whatever color she wears when she wants to feel
confident.)
(She chooses turquoise.)

OLIVIA
These are just some of the amazing characters starring in
the reading list for this year's Battle of the Books. I hope
you'll join us on this literary adventure.
(Then: You totally go off script and I don't know why but
hey . . . it's your video.)

OLIVIA (cont'd)
The thing about books . . . *(pauses . . . looks away wistfully)*

The thing about reading is it brings you into a world you can't enter any other way.

Books remind us that even though we're middle schoolers, or teachers, or whatever you are . . . words can twist, wrap, and bind us together into something that is bigger.

Bold. Creative.

If you haven't ever entered that . . . that place where it's just you, the book, and your imagination . . . you should. It's like a fresh-baked snickerdoodle . . . you want to share it.

(Um, wow. I ALMOST WANT TO READ A BOOK NOW. How'd you do that? Also . . . snickerdoodles . . . mmmm.)

(Then, video of kittens in a basket and a helicopter diving into the ocean. Because I can.)

(A chorus sings . . .)
B-b-b-book it!
(I'll Auto-Tune it for more appeal.)

Piper,

I was going to ask you to watch the twins tonight so I can go to Bunco club, but you seem really busy working for Battle of the Books. Dad said you are doing marketing or something? It's exciting to see you so pumped about reading and doing your homework!

    Anyway, keep up the hard work. I'll stay home instead. You're so creative.

                I'm proud of you. —Mom

Olivia,

I don't want you to think I'm ignoring you. I stayed up until
two a.m. working on the video, then as soon as I got home
today I worked on the video. And now it's eleven at night and
guess what I'm doing?

Ding ding ding!! Working on the video!!

Well, actually, I'm obviously writing you a note. And I'm
actually done with the video. And Olivia . . . this might be the
best thing I've ever done. And I know I haven't done a million
videos, so that isn't saying much, but for me, it's saying a lot.
This is far better than the video where I used Andrea's Barbie dolls to reenact that scene from *Love and Deception* where
Emanuel proposes to Genevieve, but then he's tragically struck
by a bus. Now he has to live out the rest of his life with a peg
leg and plays his saxophone on street corners. I have sixteen
views on that video! It's entirely possible we could get up to
thirty views on this one, Liv. THIRTY.

Now. I know you are probably sitting at home wearing a
beige sheet (or whatever your worried color is), fretting about

"What will people think!? Will it work?! Are Princess Leia buns a good look on me? Why on earth would we post this on YouTube?" (Yes, we need to put this on YouTube. Sorry.)

I need you to do something for me. I need you to trust me. Have I ever led you astray? (Please ignore all the times I have led you astray.) This video is a commercial, and we are in the business of selling reading. We have to appeal to a large audience. So maybe someone hates Star Wars but loves kittens. Or hates reading but loves a good Auto-Tune. By adding *everything* into the video, there will be *something* for everyone. Princess Leia, little houses on prairies, old dogs, teens surviving things! And most important . . . middle schoolers!

Because, really . . . it's about the books. Think about the books. (I mean, for you it's about the books. I'm just trying to sell this idea however I can. Is it working?) If this video somehow gets those books read, then we have bettered *man- and womankind.*

You might ask me to "tone it down." I get that . . . it's your standard first response to most of my ideas. But the thing is . . . you can't stop a train once it's moving. I mean, you *can* stop trains, because I think they have safety brakes, but it's probably hard and that's why trains are always tragically hitting people or dogs, as was the sad case for Buster during season nine of *Love and Deception.*

I know this is out of your comfort zone. But sometimes . . . your comfort zone has the circumfrence of a raisin. And I know I didn't spell circumfreance right, but . . . you've already done a lot of new things this year. And it worked out for you. So maybe Princess Leia buns will work out for you too.

So, again, think of literacy. And the babies and children. And the dogs. And . . . anyone you need to think of to make you upload that video. I know you're going to debate this. But please. Just do it.

Bubble letters make everything irresistible.

I also included a note my mom stuck on my door tonight along with a plate of dinner. She just knocked on the door again. Here's a script of our conversation:

MOM

Hey, Piper. You really need to get to sleep.

ME

(*Covering my computer screen*) Okay, I'm just about finished.

MOM

Can I see what you're working on?

ME

It's nothing, Mom. Just something for school.

MOM

I know. But I want to be involved. Is this assignment a
large percentage of your grade?

ME

Oh. Um. Not really.

MOM

What class is this for?

ME

(Yawning) I'm really tired, Mom.

MOM

Okay. I'll pull up your progress report in the morning.
Mrs. Fintello showed me how to do that—finally. I swear,
paper is much better than technology, but maybe that's
just the stationery store talking.

ME

(One spotlight shining down on me as I gaze into the
distance) I don't want you to see my progress report, Mom.
I'm worried you're not going to be happy. Olivia keeps
talking about catastrophic thinking, and I'm not really sure
what that means, but I might be doing it. Ever since you

said "Piper is just Piper" in the Christmas card, I've kind
of felt like I am not good enough for this family. And this
video was really fun to make and I don't want anyone to
ruin that for me. If you record over this . . . it would be like
you recorded over my heart. Or something just as dramatic.

Okay. I didn't say any of that last bit. Instead, I just shooed her out of my room. I'm totally exhausted and still really excited about the video but . . .

My grades aren't great, Olivia. They never are, but lately I just don't get it. The schoolwork. Sometimes I stare at an assignment and just kind of guess what words or numbers should go in the blanks. Having rotating classes is hard for me. Before, we had one teacher, and now there are so many and they give out homework all at the same time.

And thanks for all you said about showing my parents the video. You made some goodish points, but I just don't agree. I already know which directions this could roll. First off, they might see my progress report and tell me I need to focus on my grades more and cut out extracurricular activities like LARP and videos. Even though they've always been supportive of me and say, "we just want you to give your personal best," this might not be best enough.

Another possibility: they might see the video and *not care.*

Like what if next year, on the Christmas card, they still don't have anything to add on the Piper line? Why on earth would I put myself out there like that?

Ahem. I won't think about it. I'm too excited about this video. Tonight is a *celebration*. I'll slip you the thumb drive tomorrow so you can show it to Miss del Rosario before we upload it on YouTube. My toes are tingling right along with you. (I totally forgot to add a Jordan/Jackson FREAKOUT for you. Here you go . . .)

OLIVIA TALKED TO BOYS AND THEY WERE BOTH INTERESTED AND OUR DOUBLE WEDDING IS TOTALLY GOING TO HAPPEN AND NO WE AREN'T SERVING CARROT CAKE

You're a star,
Piper

Grateful: Our video. GOLDEN! GOLD! SHINY! SPARKLY! OSCAR-Y!

Piper,

Usually, I'm not one to say fudging the truth with your mom is a good idea. But I get it. I just wish there was a way you could show it to her and not worry about her immediately cutting out all the fun in your life.

So what I'm about to tell you is the exact events that happened today at approximately 12:14 p.m.

I was in the library during lunch. This meant Miss del Rosario and I were the only ones in there.

I sat down behind her computer and twirled in her comfy swivel chair (she told me I could). With Miss del Rosario standing behind me, I put in the thumb drive and hit play.

How do I explain what happened next?

Oh. Let's just say . . . JAW DROPPING.

Piper. The video. It's . . . amazing. Seriously amazing!!! Your parents should see this—seriously. Like, it's professional but real and funny and smart and *good*. But all that stuff I said when I went off-script was so personal. I'm not even sure where it came from. The words just flowed out of my mouth like I wasn't in control.

Maybe I said it because it's the way I really feel . . . so it didn't take any thought on my part.

Honestly, though, the idea of putting this up on YouTube gives me a nervous feeling in my stomach. The fact that we have Katniss shooting her arrow into Stanley Yelnats's hole is beyond awesome. Everyone will love it. But my heartfelt part? Yikes.

What if they laugh?

Whisper?

Make fun of me?

So all this is what I was saying to Miss del Rosario in that swivel chair. When I turned around to look at her, she wasn't biting her lip like she does when she's worried about something.

Instead Miss del Rosario was grinning from ear to ear. "I love it!!!!" She clobbered me with a hug. Clobbered me, Piper. Then she thanked me like eight thousand times. "I can't wait to show this to all the students during homeroom!"

For some reason, her using the words "all the students" made me realize: it would be seen by ALL THE STUDENTS! I mean, that was the plan all along, but *knowing it will happen for sure* is something totally worth freaking out over. I hopped up and backed away slowly. "Are you sure it's necessary to show it to *all* of them?"

She nodded. "We just need to upload it so the video can be shared with all the monitors in each classroom." Miss del Rosario held her finger over the upload button. "Ready?"

No, of course I wasn't ready. This could be a huge embarrassment for me.

I'll be called Princess Leia Buns FOREVER.

But that look on Miss del Rosario's face . . . the excitement. And then your one request from me: to trust.

Even though it feels like I'm sliding down a ride at Mustang Waterpark that is far too scary and steep for me, I think it's time to let go of the rails and fall.

So I whispered to Miss del Rosario, "Let's do this."

And guess what!

We did.

We hit

UPLOAD

(eeeeeeeek!)

Here we go, Piper . . .

Wheeeeeee!
This is terrifying!
And awesome!
And even steeper than
I imagined!
Oh well, too late now!

Your forever friend who will forever trust,

Olivia

Grateful List

1. Stepping Out

2. Of my Comfort Zone

3. For the Sake

4. Of the Greater Good

5. And all that stuff!

Olivia . . .

So I woke up this morning to check how many views we have. I know you watched it after you uploaded it yesterday with Miss del Rosario. So there is one. Then I watched it four times last night just to make sure it streamed all right. Five. But when I woke up this morning, there were four more views! Did you watch the video this morning? Or do you think those were other people? When Miss del Rosario shows it in our homerooms, we will reach double digits.

Not that I care how many people watch it. We need to get readers to sign up. I get that. Still, I've never put my work . . . my *art* out there like this.

I'm heading into homeroom now. Will write after the big premiere!

ONE GLORIOUS HOUR LATER . . .

Um. Oh my gosh. How do I say this? There are a lot of words swirling in my brain but I can't pick the best one! How do I explain what just happened?

Maybe like this: that was one of the best moments of my life. And by maybe, I mean *ABSOLUTELY*.

I sat in the middle. I figured this way I could look back and see half of the viewers' faces, but still feel like I was part of the experience. They laughed at all the right things. Some kids even called out the characters as soon as they appeared on-screen (you were maybe right about the Spider-Man costume. Still, it was funny). A guy behind me said to his friend, "Dude, maybe we should read some of these books. It's cool."

It's. Cool. I have . . . I mean, *we* have made reading cool! It probably was cool before this video, but now it's *frigid*. Also, at the very end, when you got all Bare-Your-Soul-Ish, some girls let out "awwws" and I even saw Miss del Rosario wipe at her eyes. I knew including you was a smart directorial direction.

It felt like in *Love and Deception*, in the coma scene (the third one) when Gloria Amsterdam told her dad she still loved him, even if he gave her an unnecessary face transplant during her second coma. I bawled for days after that. That's good TV, and what those kids saw today was good YouTube. The emotion was just so . . . thick in the air.

Afterward, everyone clapped. Spontaneously. Then the

lights came on and the noise got loud. Everyone was laughing and sharing their favorite parts and . . .

Olivia. I don't know how to say this. But those two minutes were . . . if not the best moment of my life, then the moment that I felt most like . . . me. I want to feel it again, over and over. I want to create more projects and entertain more viewers.

This is my thing. I want to stick this pride in my pocket and pet it for a while. *Pet, pet.* Hello, darling video. I adore you so. *Pet, pet.*

Another little note—Danny came in to drop off a library book. *Old Yeller,* actually. He said he looked over the book list when we made that first (awful) video, and thought it looked good.

"Are you doing Battle of the Books?" I asked.

He shrugged. "Nah. Too busy. I'm creating this lemonade candy to sell online, now that my lemonade-stand business is dying down."

"But then why did you read the book?" I asked.

"It's called *reading for enjoyment*. Try it some time, Pipes." He picked something off the shoulder of my sweater. I kind of flinched. I didn't mean to. He just surprised me. "Glad you bagged the other video. Your new one is much better. Star power."

My class was starting to file out of the library. "Yeah, Olivia was great in it."

"Come on, I'm talking about you. You know that." He glanced over at the display of Valentine's Day books. Miss del Rosario had paper hearts and candy with a sign that said, "Real love is a good book!"

"Have you read any of those?" he asked.

"What? No."

He picked up a copy of a book called *Cinder*. "This looks good. I'll get this next."

"That's a girl book," I said.

He looked at me weird. "Why, because there's a girl's shoe on the cover? That's dumb. *Old Yeller* is about a dog. Does that mean only dogs can read it?"

He had a point. So I said nothing. Then he waved at someone else and just walked away. No good-bye. Which is rude, right?

But what he said . . . it was kind of nice, right?

HE CONFUSES ME.

After he walked away, Miss del Rosario came over and put her hand on my shoulder. Why are people so shoulder-y in the library?

"Did you need to check out a book?" she asked.

"What? Me? Oh, no. I don't read. I mean . . . I don't need a book."

She tapped a white book with plaid on the spine. "Really? You seem to love drama. And stories."

"Well . . . yeah." I took the compliment. Because, well, I do.

"I just finished this one. It's called *I'd Tell You I Love You, but Then I'd Have to Kill You*. Have you heard of it?"

I looked at the door. Lunch was next. I am super pro-lunch. "Nope."

"It's part of the Gallagher Girls series, by Ally Carter. The first one is about a girl at a spy school who falls for an ordinary boy. Lots of scandal. Mixed messages. Betrayal. Intrigue. Complicated stuff."

I mean, I can find all that in an episode of *Love and Deception*. Still, spy school sounds sorta non-boring. "If I check it out, will you let me go?"

She laughed. "I would never force a book on anyone. I'm a matchmaker, not a bully! But you do have to read twenty minutes in class anyway, right? Might as well like what you're reading."

This was logical thinking. So I dropped the book in my backpack. Have you read it? When would I even have time to read anyway?

Also, that Valentine's display reminded me that we're only about a month away from V-Day. We'll need to discuss how this holiday is handled in Middle School Country. We have more friends now, which is great! So I'm writing out our annual Valentine's Card List, involving our friends and sorta friends and more than friends.

Which is very scientific.

ON CLOUD NINE,

Pipes

Grateful: Libraries that also serve as theaters, applause, mango salsa, cute library book displays, that new funny Doritos commercial

PIPER & OLIVIA'S
VALENTINE CARD LIST

Note: this may change at any point depending on
their behavior and our moods

FRIENDS

Ellie from Chess Club—cool girl

Bethany Livingston—gossipy but still cool

Eve—sometimes points out how overly peppy
Bethany is, so I like!

Andrea Moss—most awesome third grader ever

Our families—they live near us

Blinkie—probably has no girlfriend, poor little guy

The cast of LOVE AND DECEPTION (they just
don't know we're friends yet. Maybe this year
they'll respond to my fan mail/valentines!)

SORTA FRIENDS

Jordan Goldberg—do you know how much you mention him?

Tessa—sometimes she's kind of weird to me since she broke up with Danny

Danny Moss—I mean, he isn't our enemy

Miss del Rosario—best librarian ever!

MORE THAN FRIENDS, AKA THE LIST THAT JACKSON WHITTAKER HAS BEEN ON FOREVER, AKA THE GUYS WE WILL MARRY AT OUR DOUBLE WEDDING

Jackson Whittaker. And... yep.

McKay Davis from LOVE AND DECEPTION. I don't care if he's a character. I looooove him.

★ BETHANY'S BUSINESS ❤

HOME   NEWS   EVENTS   ABOUT   CONTACT

Hey readers/subscribers/friends/randoms/possible casting directors! Thanks for stopping by Bethany's Business! Here you'll find all the buzz happening at Kennedy Middle School. I mean, the buzz that matters. To me.

Let's get to it!

SHOUT-OUTS!

★ Lainey Willardson: WHERE DID YOU GET THAT FABULOUS CORAL LIPSTICK! I didn't even know coral was a winter color, but you wear it so well.

★ Principal Dawn: Ever since you started the Hallway Initiative, I feel like the hallway traffic has improved. I don't get bumped into my locker like before, and there is much less trash. Thank you for making our school a place conducive to learning. Not that you read this blog (unless you do? Because sometimes you smile at me with a twinkle in your eye. I know I'm a stellar student, but I'm wondering if someone clued you in to this site).

★ Jordan Goldberg: I'm still thinking about your choir performance. You should get a record deal. I'm not kidding.

WHAT IS HOT

TEA PARTIES

Like little girl tea parties. Make your own tutus, put on tons of glitter makeup, make little sandwiches in the shape of hearts and ENJOY! Tea party shops are opening up all around the country. Celebrities are all having their birthday parties in tea shops now. It's *a thing*, you guys.

YARN

Yarn is such a great fashion accessory. You can go super basic and tie a string around your finger to remind you to do something. Or braid best-friend bracelets out of yarn. Or . . . get super crafty like

Piper Jorgensen and make your own scarves. She made me a beanie for Christmas and *j'adore.*

BISTRO LIGHTING

Time for ambiance! Look, fluorescent lighting is sooooo 1985. (Well, I wasn't alive then, but the lighting is so bad in old photos!) It's bad for your pores too. So decorate your room with low lighting and kick back like it's a lounge in New York City and you're Audrey Hepburn. Glamour is IN!

BATTLE OF THE BOOKS

The awesome Miss del Rosario is heading up Battle of the Books. My friend Piper's friend Olivia made this crazy good video for it. Who knew Olivia Weston was such an innovator? My favorite part was the Star Wars introduction. And Old Yeller barking at Katniss. Oh, and that sweet part where Olivia talked about why she loves books. I loved it all, actually. Though deep down I wish Piper could have used some of the footage she shot of me since I did spend hours getting camera-ready. But! The end result of getting people to sign up for the battle is most important, so

I will swallow my pride and smile. Mom always says to "fake it till you make it" so if I smile long enough, pretty soon I'll be smiling for real.

Here's the link to the YouTube video. I've already watched it three times today.

Okay, that's all I have for now. Hook me up with some comments. I love all my readers to pieces.
LOVE, LOVE, & LOVE
Bethany

8 COMMENTS

Becca555: I am sooooo obsessed with Audrey Hepburn. I will def put up some ambiance lighting in my bistro-lounge bedroom! Peace out, Bethany!

DjTyler: Dude, can you dude this blog up a bit? I mean yarn is cool I guess. For making hacky sacks, but come on, bro! Show us dudes some diversity! Oh, and your recommendation of that video was stellar. The bomb, yo.

Bethanyblogs: Request noted, Tyler! I will attempt some dude-ish notes of interest. Though that will be quite difficult due to me being a non-dude. At least according to your implied definition of dude—can't girls be dudes too? Seems like an equal-opportunity word. Plus, boys can like yarn too. And lipstick. And whatever they want!

Danahuffhuff: That video! Incredible! I shared it on my Facebook page and then my aunt in North Carolina liked it and shared it and now all these other people I don't even know are writing comments on my Facebook post about that awesome video.

JamieheartsScience: I shared the video! My cousin in Maine shared it too!

Bethanyblogs: Keep sharing the video, Bethanites! We might convince more people to join Battle of the Books! Then we'll finally have a chance at beating Laguna Middle School . . . something that hasn't happened ever in the history of ever! Plus, Laguna's school colors are maroon and gold. Which are THE WORST.

Marketing4you: I Googled Better Business Bureau and found this. Not what I was looking for, but nicely done. You may have a future in the field of publicity and marketing.

Bethanyblogs: Wait. Did I just get famous or something? A job in marketing?! Woohoo!

Bethanyblogs: Never mind. It's spam. Ugh!

Piper,

This morning. Let me break this down . . .

The video.

Honestly, I didn't know how they reacted to it because I asked for a hall pass before the video played. I hung out in the girls' bathroom counting missing ceiling tiles.

I tried to sneak back into class, but Mr. Kunkel greeted me at the door and patted me on the back. "Nice job."

"On entering the room?" I asked.

He laughed. "The video. The students loved it."

I thanked Mr. Kunkel and turned around to face the class. Everyone was looking at me. Everyone. They were smiling, Piper. My face turned Jolly Rancher red and my feet went numb. Thankfully, Bethany hopped up and escorted me back to my seat. She whispered in my ear, "That video was like totally awesome. Everyone is talking about you. Let's do lunch sometime, okay?"

SOOOOO THAT WAS WEIRD.

And now you're telling me that people actually laughed, and awwww-ed, and clapped? This is all so . . . unbelievable.

The bell rang and I quickly gathered my things and power-walked out of there before anyone could talk to me.

Pulling my books in tight, I focused on the door at the end of the hall, history class. But I couldn't help but notice the people passing me weren't just passing me. They were looking at me. Smiling. Doing a double-take. Some guy I don't even know gave me a thumbs-up. I'm positive there are rules against all this in the Hallway Initiative. Ellie gave me a quick hug and said, "Awesome," which was totally fine since *I know her personally.* But then Vivian Wong, the captain of the eighth-grade basketball team, patted my shoulder and said, "Way to go, Katniss."

It was nice. But I had no idea what to say. This type of thing doesn't happen to me every day. I flashed her a brief smile, then sped up. *Get to class. Get to class. All this attention is super weird!* But all that speeding up didn't stop a certain someone from tracking me down in the hall.

"Olivia! Wait up!"

It was Jordan. (Should he be moved up to the friends list? Also, remember when we only had each other on that list? Oh, how we've grown!) He has smiled at me seven times this week. I counted. And now there I was, in the middle of the crowded hallway, faced with smile number eight.

"What's up?" I said super casually, because I'm a super casual girl. (Stop laughing.)

"That video was the bomb!" He smiled.

I smiled. Then I said the following: "Yeah, it was the bomb dot com!"

Oh, Piper. Why do you let me go out in public? Just keep me locked up in a cage and save me the misery. The bomb dot com?! What is wrong with me?! I blame those reruns on TV where they say those things and then there's fake laughter. There's a reason why those shows use fake laughter. Because it's not that funny.

Jordan nodded and pressed his lips together in a way that said, "Wow, I really feel sorry for you that you're saying such bizarre after-school rerun lines that were cool like seven years ago but I'm going to try and be nice about this."

I'm pretty sure that's what he was saying to me with that look.

Anyway.

"Cool." He waved bye to me as he went left and I went right.

This afternoon. Let me break this down . . .

When I got home from school, I opened the front door and surprise! Jason was standing in the kitchen eating a mayonnaise sandwich.

"What's up, munchkin?" He ruffled my hair.

I hate when he does that but I also love when he does that.

I lightly punched him on the shoulder. "Why are you here? Did you take a wrong turn?"

"Haha. I'm here for the weekend. Mom and Dad thought it would be fun to surprise you."

"Awesome! I love surprises!" Piper, you know how much I hate surprises. Being prepared is my favorite way to be. And now here I was faced with a surprise visit from my brother, who may not come back to visit from college in who knows how long and I want to hang out with him. But I need to work on my history report and I want to re-re-read my Battle of the Books books. How am I going to fit all this in?

He grabbed his car keys. "Mom and Dad won't be home for a while." He smirked. "Let's go to my favorite place."

They don't have a Dairy Queen in his college town and whenever he comes home he immediately heads there for their famous double-scoop hot-fudge sundae.

I dropped my books on the kitchen table. "Let's go."

So there we were, a mere three bites into our mountain-size sundaes, when the door flung open.

And that's when I heard the herd. A large group of giggling girls bombarded the counter.

"We need five Oreo Blizzards—stat!" Dana Huffington slapped her hands on the counter—obviously she was their designated speaker. Dana doesn't ever seem to give me the time of day. But suddenly she turned toward me, and waved. Waved?

She stuck a wad of money in her friend's hand and charged over to me. Jason and I were quietly scarfing down ice cream, so her sudden high-pitched words made us both jump a little.

Dana scooted into the booth with me and placed her hand on my shoulder. She said words. *Nice* words. "Olivia, that video was AH-MAY-ZING! I'm dying to join the battle!"

"You're going to join?"

I figured the girl never read anything other than Blogs about Lip Gloss. I like being wrong sometimes.

"We're all going to join." It was Tatiana, her other friend. All the girls had charged up to us and began to nod and agree and say things like, "We can't wait for the next meeting! When is it?"

Jason kicked at me under the table because I had apparently gone mute. This whole situation seemed to steal all the words from my mouth. Luckily, thanks to my brother's kick, I was able to form a sentence. "It's Monday, during lunch."

When a kick from your brother is a good thing. →

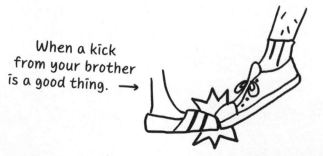

"Can't wait!" Dana said, then she jumped up and the herd disappeared into the night in a billowy cloud of fog. Not really, but I like how dramatic that sounded.

But did you notice something? There were five girls who agreed to join. Five!

That means one thing, Piper: we have saved Battle of the Books.

Sooooo . . . job well done, friend! Let's leave the video up, just in case a few more people watch it. Who knows, we may even get a couple more people to join.

Jolly Rancher red-faced but (sort of) dealing with it,
Olivia

Gratefuls:

1–5. The FIVE girls who agreed to join the battle!

Hi, Ms. Jorgensen! Can I text with Piper for a few minutes?

Sure, but only a few. She has to do homework and laundry and help me with the twins' bath.

'K! Thx!

'Sup?

Your mom works you hard!

It's like I'm living on a farm. But instead of cows, we have toddlers.

I will feel sorry for you later. Right now I have news!

Lay it on me.

My dad got a call tonight from North Dakota!

From Santa?

Not the North Pole, just North Dakota. It was my uncle.

Aaaaaand?

At first they talked about weather. They talked about weather for a long time because I think it's important to people in the Dakotas.

Aaaaaaand?

My uncle saw a link to a video on Facebook. It was my video. OUR VIDEO!

Whoa!

And my uncle said it has over 300 views. That can't be right? Is it?!

. . . please hold . . .

No. Way.

What??!!!!

I just checked it. 374 views.
Wait . . . 375.

This thing is getting around.
People are watching it! Even
in the northern part of the
country!!

Now it's at 377.

Stop hitting the refresh button
or I'm going to have a panic
attack. There must be an
explanation.

379. Ooops, didn't see your last
text. Your fingers move so fast!

It's probably just some people in my family watching it. Except that wouldn't explain why there are hundreds of views. My family's not that big. Maybe if it was YOUR family it would make sense.

My family doesn't even know about the video.

Yeah, about that. I don't get why you don't tell them. Of course they'll think it's amazing. And they're going to find out about it at some point.

No, they won't. My dad only watches reruns of detective TV shows and my mom doesn't even know how to turn a computer on most of the time.

Well, fine. You can probably take it down then, just to be sure they don't see it.

They don't even know what YouTube IS, Liv. And just because I don't want them to view it right now doesn't mean I don't want others to view it! That's why videos are online. To be viewed, hopefully by people you aren't related to. Deep breath. We will survive.

And by survive, I mean jump up and down with joy! 382 views, baby! Let's keep it up for a while and see how high it gets.

I don't know . . .

I'll give you a hug.

Not enough.

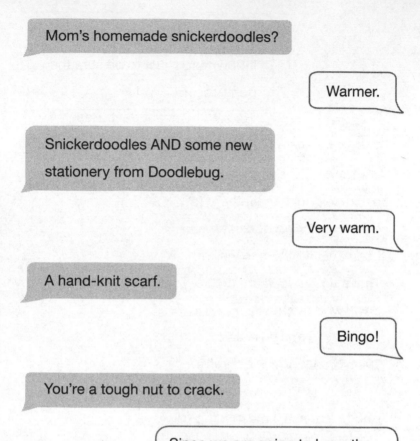

Or another option is to just ask the boy if he'd sign up.

He said he might do it. Besides, asking him would take guts; those are things I do not have.

If I find any extra guts lying around here I'll loan them to you.

Eww.

Well, this video might turn that "might" into "mighty."

What does that mean?

It means leave the video up. Gotta bolt, Mom's calling. I'm erasing texts on Mom's phone so print them out for the notebook if you want.

Have fun milking the cows!

MOOOOOOO

Piper,

I now present to you this week's episode of . . . . . .

STRANGE PHONE CALLS I RECEIVED FROM BOYS ON A RANDOM THURSDAY NIGHT.

So there I was, innocently working on my math homework and munching on sunflower seeds. Dividing fractions requires lots of snacking. I was on my fifth problem when the phone rang. I ignored it.

It rang.

I ignored.

This is how it works in the Weston household. No one answers the phone until the caller ID robot voice announces the name of the caller. We get so many calls from spammers that we hardly ever pick up.

But a few seconds later, there was a tap at my door. Mom didn't even wait for me to grant her access to my room. She just suddenly appeared with UFO-size eyes and her hand cupped over the receiver. "It's for you," she whispered.

Her eyes, her whispering . . . it was all so weird. What was going on? She never acts like this when Aunt Martha calls.

"It's . . . a *boy*." She said "boy" like she was allergic to the word.

I snatched the phone and pushed Mom back out of my room, slamming the door on her. Accidentally! I think!

"Hello?"

"Hi, is this Olivia?"

"Yes, this is she. Her. This is Olivia." How are you supposed to answer that question in a grammatically correct way? Why don't they teach us this in school?! It's like the ONE time I needed grammar skills to be on my side.

"Hey, this is Jackson."

Omgomgomgomg!

Jackson was calling me.

JACKSON.

Was calling.

MEEEEEEEEEEEEE.

My heart stopped momentarily.

"It's Jackson Whittaker . . . from your math class."

"Oh, um, hi!" It hit me that I didn't respond when he said his name. Maybe all my silence was coming off as casual-cool. Maybe not.

"Have you started the homework yet?"

"Yes." Yes? That's the best response I could come up with?

"So I don't understand it and my mom said I should call someone in the class."

"Okay, I can help you with that." Aaaaaand now I sound like a bank teller. How would you like me to cash your check—twenties or hundreds?

"How do I divide the fraction? Like what goes into what number?"

"You don't divide anything, actually. You multiply the reciprocal."

"Is that French?"

How adorable is he? Answer: adorable to the millionth degree. "You flip the second fraction and multiply."

"Multiply what?"

"Across. The tops then the bottoms."

"Ohhhhhh, I get it."

So now we have arrived at the big moment. The real reason Jackson was calling me. Was he going to tell me he wanted to join the battle? Did he want to know what type of candy I'd like in my valentine? Or did this have something to do with the Spring Dance? It seemed pretty early to start asking dates. And do sixth graders even *go* on dates to spring dances? Oh, I really hope Bethany blogs about this topic soon.

"So, that's cool," he said. "Thanks and stuff . . ."

"Um—"

"Yeah? Were you going to say something?"

Was I? I thought this was where he said things in a romantic fashion. "I . . . um . . . just forgot what I was going to say."

"Oh."

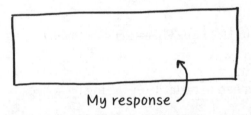

My response

That blank space above represents the large hole in our conversation that consisted of neither one of us talking.

I finally broke out of that empty rectangle. "Soooo, I'll see you in class tomorrow?"

"Sure, and um—"

"Yes?"

"That video about Battle of the Books was . . . cool."

Have you ever heard a more amazing adjective than cool? It's, well, the coolest adjective out there. "Really?"

"Um, yeah. Bye."

"Umm . . ."

Click.

Holy macaroni. WHAT WAS THAT??? Was that a flirty I-will-ask-you-to-the-dance-and-give-you-a-valentine-and-join-the-battle call? That boy is all sorts of confusing. And nerve-racking. But in a good way, I think. And we've made more progress in the last couple months than in our entire (nonexistent) relationship. I hope he likes gold and blush as colors for the double wedding. They're neutral but elegant, you know?

But, wait. Hold up. This story isn't over.

Ring!

I knew it had to be Jackson calling back because for macaroni's sake I didn't even get a chance to say good-bye!

"Olivia?"

"Yeah?"

"It's your favorite person. Or at least, the guy who admires your spelling skills."

Jordan.

I laughed. He's always telling me correct spelling is my superpower.

"That's me, Captain Speller!" I even had a hand on my hip, superhero style.

"Wonder Woman Speller . . . to the rescue!"

"Princess Proper Speller . . . here to save the day!"

And then we just started laughing and he told me he just rewatched the new Star Wars movie and I told him all about my favorite YouTube video (besides ours, of course).

"Oh! Is it the one where cats play patty-cake?"

He's good. "That's my second favorite."

"Cats jumping on ceiling fans?"

"No. But those are always entertaining. And slightly violent."

"Cats with fake mustaches?"

I laughed. "Cats knocking stuff over!"

"Oh, I love that one! We should make one where we line up a bunch of objects—"

"—and I could set my cat, Blinkie, next to them—"

"—and you tell him to clean up—"

"—and he knocks it all over until the table is cleared—"

"—and the crowd goes wild!"

I haven't laughed that hard in a while. We talked a little bit longer. I told him about Blinkie's blinking abilities and he told me about his salamander who only eats Thai food. Then Jordan started acting like a robot and hung up. It was weird and hysterical. Especially because he never even said why he was calling.

But are you counting, Piper? I got two phone calls from boys. On a Thursday.

WHAT DOES THIS MEAN?

At least our video gave me and Jackson something to talk about other than math. Progress! Right?

All phoned out,

Olivia

Gratefuls:

1. Thursdays
2. Phone calls on Thursdays
3. Possibly flirty phone calls on a Thursday
4. Receiving TWO possibly flirty calls on a Thursday
5. Ending a phone call with a boy who is acting like a robot

Olivia,

Go back in this notebook. Way back. Back to the note I wrote for you so you could muster up the courage to talk to Jackson. Read that. Now pat yourself on the back. Because that was only a few months ago, and now look how far you've come!! Three conversations with Jackson in only a few weeks! I'm pretty sure he's going to propose any day now.

Which doesn't really work for our double-wedding plan, since my imaginary future husband presently lives in Portland and is the editor of his high school newspaper. Yes, he's a bit older, and yes, I still love him even though he's bookish. He also eats a lot of sushi. Of this I'm quite sure. His name is . . . Camden Giasponi. Hold on. I'm adding him to a list . . .

MORE THAN FRIENDS
Jackson Whittaker, aka Chatty McChatterson
Camden Giasponi. Or a soap star. I'll think about it

So maybe you should slow things down with Jackson so I can have time to grow up, graduate college, and meet Vaughn (I just re-decided his name is Vaughn) on a humanitarian trip. At the rate you're going, you and Jackson will have seven kids by then.

Or maybe you and Jordan? Because . . . um, look. I know you had that note debacle last year where Jordan got a note meant for Jackson. And so Jordan thinks you like him. And obviously he likes you. But maybe that isn't a totally bad thing? He's sort of cute and Bethany thinks he is a star, and don't you think it's kind of weird that you finish each other's sentences like that? I might not know much about crushes (although I know plenty about forbidden romance thanks to *Love and Deception*), but I do know that when you find people who are cool to be around, you should probably keep being around them.

Hold on . . .

MORE THAN FRIENDS
Jackson (duh)

Camden/Vaughn/Reginald (I really like that name too. He sounds like a duke)

Jordan Goldberg??

I know you told me to add him to the "friends" list, but I'm upgrading him.

You know, this kind of reminds me of when Cammie goes to the town carnival and meets Josh in *I'd Tell You I Love You, but Then I'd Have to Kill You*. Like she feels like her life is supposed to be one way, but then BOOM, she meets a boy.

Oh yeah. I'm reading that book Miss del Rosario gave me. Like she said, I have to read anyway, and I used to just stare at the wall, so I started her book. I've only read a bit but I do think I'm understanding boys a little better. And spy technology. And maybe I've already figured out the ending, but I do have a deep understanding of story elements thanks to my show.

Where were we? Right. I bet Jackson is just as nervous to talk to you as you are to him. Did he *really* need help with homework? Doubt it.

Speaking. Of. Homework.

Here's my progress report . . .

Student Progress Report
Kennedy Middle School

Student: Piper Jorgensen   Year: 6th Grade   Quarter: 3rd

COURSE	GRADE
MATH	C
SOCIAL STUDIES	D+
FRENCH	B-
ENGLISH	B
LITERATURE	C

That D is not going to sit pretty with my parents. Or the Cs serving as the bread in my mediocre grade sandwich. Obviously, they won't print out these grades to slap on our fridge. I'm nervous to even get a parent signature.

I talked to Felicity about it today at LARP. We had our first meeting of the year and I got to play the mad scientist character. I think I'm moving up in LARP. Last time I was a rug. Yes, that was a real character and not like a magical flying carpet. I just had to lie down and look carpetish. The Game Master still doesn't like me much.

The whole time I just kept sharing my Master! Plans! and then shaking my head when no one understood my genius. I know my character was a little cliché, but you couldn't help but envy her. She knows too much for her own good. Her brain is just sprouting with all this information, and everyone around her is much more simple, and she's so frustrated that people don't think like her.

In real life, the mad scientist would probably hate me. I saw this YouTube video once about cool chemical combos, so I made a baking soda volcano. My dad thought I was a future scientist, so he bought me all these books. Now those books are the stand for my laptop when I make not-science videos. That mad scientist would shake her fist and say, "Knowledge at your fingertips! People would give their lives to learn that knowledge and you're making a story about three-legged dancing cats! Tragedy!"

Or maybe mad scientists have a deep appreciation for well-thought-out videos with trained animals, I don't know.

Anyway, Felicity came up to me afterward and gave me a chocolate rose. Which was sorta like a cheesy reality dating show, but I'm not going to argue with chocolate.

"What's this for?" I asked.

"For being director of the year," Felicity said. "I saw the revised movie. Great call going in a new direction."

"Thanks. Sorry . . . sorry the first video didn't work."

She waved her hand in the air. "That's showbiz. Besides, I'm behind in school and my parents want me to cut back on auditioning."

"Really? Me too. I just got my progress report. It . . . wasn't great."

"Grades are the worst invention on earth. Well, after tests." Felicity smiled at me. "But you . . ." She poked me on the shoulder. ". . . *you* have talent. Serious skills, girl."

It was, like, the perfect thing I needed to hear at the perfect time I needed to hear it.

HAPPY SIGH . . .

And our video is a hit! I wonder how many views we have on YouTube now. . . .

Piper

GRATEFUL: Video views, how you and Jordan are like Ashley and McKay in *L&D* and you don't even know it, pretending like my grades don't exist (grades? What grades?), black nail polish

Hey, I know you have the notebook, but I was just in the computer lab reading Bethany's blog. (Shut up. I know I read it too much. I'm supporting a friend, that's it.) I checked the number of views on the video, just for kicks and giggles, and it's up to 409!! Wow, Bethany isn't kidding about BUZZ.

Hey, just got home. And...it's 890...how on earth did it double in just a few hours? Is someone watching it over and over again?

HEY—um...I'm about to go to sleep. And it's in the thousands. It's up to 3,493. Who is watching it? Are there a lot of Spider-Man fans in north Dakota sharing this? Liv, what's happening here?

OJ

apples   yogurt

crackers   mayo

popcorn   bananas

pita   corn flakes

HEY HEY HEY HEY HEY.
Just woke up. 9,023. Liv, I'm
freaking out. What is going on?
Did the internet break overnight?

Liv.
Liv.
Liv.
Liv.
Forget North Dakota. I just checked in
the computer lab. You have 34,239
views. Something happened. I don't
know what happened. But this
happening is the biggest happening...
ever. LIV. WHAT HAPPENED?

~~~~~~

Dear Bomb-Dot-Com (sorry, I had to),

I think I have it. I found this note on the floor after class today.
And this really is the biggest happening since time began. I . . .
I have no words . . .

(Ignore that part, Olivia. I mean, Olive.)

OMG, did you hear about that Olive girl?

NO. TEXT ME!

I can't! Principal Dawn is acting cray-cray about phones.
It's part of the Hallway Initiative. Anyway, so this girl, Olive,
made this YouTube video about a history club or something.
Anyway, then that author Juan Verde saw it and thought
it was cool so he tweeted it. You know who he is—he wrote
that book about two kids who have a rare disease so they're
sent on a space shuttle before they die and they fall in love.
Doesn't sound like much of a romantic comedy, but it is.
The guy's got talent.

ISN'T THAT A MOVIE?

How do you think I know about it? The book? Ha. Anyway, so
Juan Verde has like a gazillion followers, and they're all book
people. So this is like a cause for them now.

**A CAUSE FOR WHAT? WHAT DO THEY CARE ABOUT A
HISTORY VIDEO?**

Maybe it was a read-more-books video. I don't remember.
The little cat in a basket was cute though. Anyway Olive is
totally famous now and we go to school with her.
So let's meet her so she can make us famous too.

I DON'T THINK IT WORKS THAT WAY.

Just text me later. Ugh, all this note writing hurts my hand.
Sooooooo old-fashioned.

WAY VINTAGE. IT'S SORT OF COOL.

And . . . that's it. Don't ask me who wrote this note. I don't
know and it doesn't matter. This is what the faceless masses
are saying, Liv. 34,595 views.

I was excited when the *Love and Deception* trailer I made
with the twins went to double digits. I can't believe something I
created is getting so much coverage! Juan Verde tweeted it, Liv.

JUAN. AMAZING. VERDE.

Are we famous? Now my brain is stirring with all the possible follow-up videos. Maybe we can create a web series of
your actual book team? Do one-on-one interviews with each

of the characters . . . sorry, *members*. I can sneak in and document what other schools are doing to prepare. Is there some really rich school or snobby Battle of the Books team I can villainize? I want to cast you as the underdogs. Everyone loves an underdog.

I hope Jackson joins now. And it's so good that Jordan and Bethany joined, since she's totally in love with him. OOOOOOHHH!! Drama! I'll have to catch that on film. I'll put it into a montage with some music. Pop music would cost me money . . . I wonder what stock instrumentals I can find online.

Look at me. Thinking out loud. Thinking on paper, actually. But this isn't about the film (mostly). It's about the exposure to . . . you know . . . literacy. Which is what this is all about. And also the children. And global warming! And . . .

➡ BABY SEALS!! ⬅
Not really, but OMG the cuteness

Wow . . . I'm already writing my Emmy acceptance speech. Now there are 41,292 views! Whoa!! I wonder if my parents will hear about this—probably not. They're so Internet Out of It, they probably don't know who Juan Verde is. So we're, like, safe.

Okay, speaking of my parents, I need to transition now. I'm going to use some new stationery my mom just got me from her store and paste it in here. I think the dove gray is brooding. I need to brood. (Brooding means moody but in a deep and poetic way on gray-colored paper, right? Did I use that word right?)

I gave Mom my progress report. She called the school and asked for parent conferences with all my teachers. And all my teachers said things like I'm a "fair" student, or I "could excel if I applied myself."

So. Guess who now has a tutor?
I don't know yet who my tutor will be. But I do know my mom wants me to meet with him/her three days a week. Which is the real issue here.
Not the grades.

We have some schedule conflicts.
"But what about LARP and the animal shelter?" I asked.
"You'll just have to pick what you want to cut back," my mom said.

Liv, it's like saying I just have to pick which arm to cut off. Probably my left because I'm right-handed, but I'm really attached to my left arm too.
Get it? Attached. Where is the grade for humor, America?

I'll do both. I'll show them I can do it all. I mean, yes, I don't always understand everything in school. And yes . . . I've been spending a lot of time thinking about this video. I don't blame my parents... they are being parents. Luke and Talin are so perfect, they've never had any kids with school problems before. In this family, getting Cs (and okay... a D) is suddenly this huuuuuuuggggggeeee crisis. Normal is abnormal. Piper is just ... Piper.

Also, I think Andrea told me Danny had a tutor a few years ago. Should I ask him about it? Maybe he can help me look at things from a business angle. I do know this—my parents for sure can't find out about the video, or they'll say my grades are bad because I'm spending too much time obsessing about that. Which isn't true. Mostly.

Before I started writing you (and while I wrote you, as the grease on this paper will prove), I ate two bags of jalapeño potato chips. And I've checked the YouTube views a few more times. You're going to hit 50k by morning. Those two random girls are right. You're totally famous now. So excited to work with you on future projects. (Respected directors say sentences like that.)

Tons of xoxoxo,
Pipe

Grateful: Juan, Verdddeeee, creative validation, YouTube likes, a glass of milk because those potato chips were spicy

Juan Verde
@officialjuanverde

✔ Follow

Whoa. This girl nailed it. Why books are important . . . with some laughs. I promise you will want to pick up a book after watching this . . . www.bitly.sdklsjdf.pbu

10:02 PM

↩ ⇄ 1.2k ♥ 5k

Whaaaat? Are we famous?
Can we buy limos with hot tubs now?

Piper,

I checked the internet. And OMG . . .

Need oxygen, need oxygen.

You were right. Juan Verde tweeted about our video.

JUAN.

VERDE!!!

I've read all of his books, not just the one that was made into a movie. He's in my top fifteen authors who are still alive! (Don't get me started on the dead ones because that's kind of a downer and I want to keep feeling giddy like this for a while!)

I guess I was worried about us being teased for the video ("us" meaning "me"). But if it's being viewed by book people, like *actual people who read and write books*, then . . . this is awesome. A dream come true, Piper.

So I can't imagine that things could get better, but guess what! They got better!

I have to tell you about this morning—near my locker. It

was one for the books. If the book is titled *All the Awesome Things*.

"Olivia! Over here!" It was Dana Huffington. Standing. Waving. She was with her sister. Her sister who is in *eighth grade*!

"See, Darla? I do know her. Olivia, come meet my sister." Darla Huffington. I'd seen her around, of course, but she's like the sun—you don't look right at her. She's too sparkly for that. And there she was, smiling and knowing that I exist.

It looked like Darla's locker was the cool eighth graders' hangout spot in between classes. I was greeted with smiles and laughter and then they all talked to me at once and it was all one big blob of awesome conversation—one where I didn't even have to say a word, just smile and nod. No one even seemed all that concerned with the Hallway Initiative and how we're not supposed to gather in groups. Maybe the Hallway Initiative didn't even *apply* to them?

In the past it had bothered me when groups of people blocked the lockers with their socializing because you had to fight to get in the middle and finally, finally get to your bottom locker except there wasn't any air to breathe once you got there. The whole situation was survival of the fittest. Like a salmon swimming upstream to Alaska or something.

At least I'm not trying to get to a locker in a middle school!

Anyway, this time it didn't seem to bother me so much. Why? Because the following words were said to me:

"Olivia, that video . . . it's so amazing!"

"You're the funniest, OMG."

"Where'd you find that adorable bonnet?"

"And then the Auto-Tuning . . . brilliant."

It went on and on like that and just before the bell rang, I asked them if they would all join the battle and come to our meeting today at lunch.

"YES!!!"

So that's seven more people.

This is all so exciting. It's entirely possible that since I just added seven people, we may have more than twelve people show up. I need a bigger box of donuts! And more teams!

Ms. Benson will be so excited to hear about this. It's the power of positive thoughts. Think them and positive things will happen. I should chart this in my emotion journal.

Wow, there's a lot to do to get ready for this meeting. It won't be easy because of that history paper I have to write. And I'm going to skip Chess Club today. Getting all this done in between after-school activities and homework assignments is tricky. You probably get how hard all this is, especially since your parents are saying the T word. Tutor.

I know what you mean when you say it's weird to talk about something so great and suddenly shift to something that's not so great. Life is weird like that.

It reminds me of that time when we were driving home from Nana's funeral. We were all wearing black and our faces were tear-stained. But despite all that sadness, we were hungry. So we stopped by Wendy's to get Frosties and french fries (Nana's favorite treat). The cashier took our order then happily said to us, "So how's your day going?"

There was really no way to answer that question.

Fine?

Horrible?

Do you really not see our puffy red faces and black clothing?!

None of us said anything. Which was weird . . . and suddenly we broke out in laughter. Laughter that made us all start to cry again.

But in a good way.

I don't know why, but it felt like the biggest relief in the world to laugh while eating Nana's favorite treat.

Sometimes the good and normal part of our lives intersects the bad. Things always seem to crisscross, like a spider web.

So. The tutor. I'm not sure it's a bad thing. Your parents probably want to make sure they're doing whatever they can to make you successful. If *you* do good, *they* feel good. Parents are so wrapped up in what we do and don't do. Sheesh.

I mean, your grades don't have to be connected to LARP, videos, knitting. You can still succeed in school and have hobbies. So if that's what you're really worried about—don't be. The tutor will help. And your parents will like the video.

Stop it. Don't argue with me. I can hear you arguing.

I know you say that the good stuff you do isn't refrigerator-worthy. And maybe you don't have the best past with videos. Yes, they taped over your memory card. True, they laughed (and not in a good way) at your video about Barbies and Sudden Blindness that you made with Andrea. (I loved how you turned it into a story about valuing inner beauty, not the beauty you can see on the outside. Brilliant.) Sure, they do seem pretty consumed with your siblings' activities.

But this is different.

I even tested the video out on my parents. They loved it! And then Mom made some of her famous sweet cornbread and we got in my bed and snacked while we watched it over and over. Mom always says, "You aren't a true Southerner until you have cornbread crumbs in your bed." I'm not sure if that's some sort of metaphor, but I'm guessing I don't understand it because I was raised in California, not Atlanta. Sometimes I think she forgets that I'm not *actually* Southern.

Anyway, the point is I stuck my head out of my shell and I told my parents about it. The world didn't end, they weren't mad, it was totally fine.

Maybe things are finer than you think.

You'll see, when you come to the meeting. (You are coming, right?)

I keep going over who might come and I've come up with my team . . .

Me (of course)

Bethany (the girl is gossipy but the girl can read)

Jordan (his enthusiasm is contagious—although this is just about literary enthusiasm, because I don't really think of him *that way*, so you can move him back to the friends list and keep Jackson in the crush spot he's held forever)

Possibly Jackson if he signed up. He probably doesn't even know who Juan Verde is, so I'm not sure *all* my dreams will come true. But today has been pretty close to perfect. It's crazy that he still gives me butterflies in my stomach. By the way, why is that romantic?

I tried to draw a butterfly-filled stomach and . . . ew. Let's move on.

I can't wait to walk into that meeting and find myself surrounded with people excited to read and talk about books. And get this . . . Mom said she'd wait in line at Krispy Kreme and get a bunch of warm donuts. She plans to drop them off at the school at lunchtime. This will be all sorts of amazing.

Oh! And T-shirt design! Our school must have matching T-shirts. Maybe I can get my dad to help me sketch something out. How about a girl with Katniss braids holding a book in one hand, a shovel in the other, standing in a hole next to Old Yeller with a caption that says, "The Battle Has Begun!" But I'm not sure how we can incorporate Laura Ingalls Wilder's bowl of oatmeal. Also, I don't think she ever actually ate oatmeal in the book.

Eeek! I can smell those Krispy Kremes already . . .

Olivia

Grateful:

1. JUAN

2. VERDE

3. Juan Verde's Twitter followers

4. The orange sorbet cones that Dad and I ate yesterday afternoon while we sat on the benches outside Rite-Aid and soaked up the sun as I told him all about how we made the video

5. OUR BATTLE OF THE BOOKS MEETING WHERE WE WILL ALL DISCUSS OUR LOVE OF BOOKS AND THERE MAY POSSIBLY BE A DOZEN PEOPLE THERE!!! omg omg omg life is so good sometimes.

Olivia,

This is all so exciting! Like way better than the annual Yarn Hut clearance sale. I feel like Cammie when she goes on her first Covert Operations mission in *I'd Tell You I Love You, but Then I'd Have to Kill You*. By the way, I'm on page fifty. It doesn't remind me of a book, if that makes sense. Like when I read it, it plays out like a movie, which I like.

But, of course, videos (and *Love and Deception*) are much better . . . I mean, personally appealing, which is why I'm never going to do BoB. Even if my parents sort of think I'm doing it. And sort of I am, just not in the way they think.

And that's all we're going to talk about that for now. See? I'm not arguing. Just . . . refocusing our topic of conversation.

So of course I'm coming today! There was no way I was going to direct such a critically acclaimed (or at least mass-viewed) video and not follow up on the rest of the creative experience. That's why I brought the camera to today's lunch meeting. Because the more I think about developing this

project, the more I think that maybe . . . just hear me out . . .
we need to highlight the **BATTLE** part more.

This story has soooo much potential for conflict! I mean,
it's war! (With books and school and learning and stuff.)

More soon!

~P

Dear Olivia,

Here is the script of two interviews I videotaped today at the meeting:

P

BETHANY LIVINGSTON:
CAN YOU BELIEVE HOW MANY PEOPLE
ARE HERE?!

(Director's note: You know I love Bethany, but her exclamation points make my ears bleed sometimes. I bet if I let the blood drip long enough, it would form an exclamation point on my cheek.)

Seriously, so many people! Like everybody who is anybody and then some bodies who are just like...

bodies. But super helpful bodies! I think we can totally win it this year, and I've done it every year since it started. I was on the second-place team in fourth grade. Did I tell you that?

(Director's note: THREE TIMES.)

Anyway, before it was just, like, booky people. And now there are people who aren't so booky, but this is like expanding their horizons and stuff! It's great to see a certain "someone" joined. I'm talking about Jordan, of course.

(Director's note: she blushed here.)

And then Jackson Whittaker showed up too. Shocker! But cool.

(Director's note: Did you just about faint when he walked through the door? Remember: if you ever feel fainty due to a boy walking through a door, just pinch yourself—the pain distracts you. SO I'VE HEARD.)

Then Olivia's mom dropped off warm donuts. We didn't even get the cast-off donuts, like powdered lemon creme, which are ew.

(Director's note: I'd totally eat one.)

MY VOICE:
(Which I will cut out, because I want the director to be invisible.)
Soooo... why did you join Battle of the Books again?

BETHANY:
Oh yeah. Well, duh. Because I always do. My mom says the everyday curriculum isn't challenging enough for me, and even though we are always petitioning for more gifted education, they can only provide so much. So I'm always looking for supplemental learning, and this is one of my supplements! And I love books. I'm writing my own. Someday. Or I'll just use my blog as a springboard for a memoir. You'll be in it, Piper! Isn't that fabulous?

(Director's note: as your Southern mother would say, bless her heart.)

OWEN MEEKERSON, aka BARRY DOTTER:
(Remember this kid? He tried to change his name to Barry in fourth grade because he's obsessed with Harry Potter and it rhymes?) Man. This group. Am I right?

DIRECTOR:
What do you mean? (Because . . . vague much?)

OWEN:
I mean, I don't know how these groups are going to come together. We haven't really discussed our strengths and weaknesses yet. I'm a fantasy guy, so I should pair up with someone who loves contemporary or horse books. So when we get asked questions, we can cover all our bases. But look. Those girls over there (he pointed to the Bethanites), they all just like teen romance. And all the Potterites are together, and I love those dudes, but it's not like Harry Potter is a Battle of the Book book. So you asked if I think this

P

is going well? Not really. But the donuts are good. I'd come again for the warm donuts.

Whatever, Barry. Go put on an invisibility cloak or something. Not to editorialize, but I personally thought the meeting was a smash, and there is so much material. Like two girls were arguing over whether they should do a spin-off group and call it Battle of the Magazines, because one girl loves US WEEKLY and the other one is totally team PEOPLE. I don't know what they would get quizzed on— who really wore it best? Still, they seem passionate and that's what I want to document. I would have recorded that interaction, but my camera battery died. Curse you, technology!! (Just kidding. I love you, technology. Please don't ever leave me. Also, I love you, notebook, even if you are NOT technology. I love many things.)

RANDOM NOTES FROM FIRST MEETING OF BATTLE OF THE BOOKS

FORTY: Number of students. If you have four on each team plus one alternate, that's EIGHT teams. (I know you know that math already. Still, isn't that cool that I applied math knowledge to real life?) Bodies bodies bodies. It was like the Library Vampire Apocalypse, minus the vampires or the apocalypse, but still in a library. Also, remember when they tried to turn soap hero McKay Davis into a vampire in season eleven of Love and Deception? There was such a revolt, they had to hurry and switch the plotline so that he wasn't a vampire after all, he was just anemic. But where was I again?

TEN: Number of books. How is anyone able to read ten books? Liv, honestly, I don't think I've ever read a book all the way through. Not ever. The letters just kind of become blurry after a couple of paragraphs. I can read the words, but I lose the ability/interest to understand what the words are telling me. Add in meaning and themes and all the other stuff you're supposed to look for, and it's so much work. Except for this book I'm reading, of course. Not that it counts.

NINETEEN: The number of main characters in LOVE AND DECEPTION. I could tell you the ages, names, character arcs, and love interests of all nineteen. Why can't one of the books on that list be about LOVE AND DECEPTION? Sorry, that didn't have much to do with anything. I was just proving a point.

THREE: Number of times Miss del Rosario cried when she discussed literature. Look, the dog is always going to die in the story. That shouldn't be a shock, lady. Sorry if that sounded mean. She is very nice and I can see why you like her. I just don't think I can ever introduce her to LOVE AND DECEPTION. That has some emotionally potent stuff in there. The episode where Randall Menard revealed he was raised in a cave by thieves and that's where his evilness started left me WEEPING.

But then again, Miss del Rosario did introduce me to that book that I am sort of somewhat almost reading.

FOUR: Number of shots I got of Jackson Whittaker! If I don't use them in the documentary, I'll just make a montage for you to use for romance purposes. He always has his forehead scrunched up like he's confused. Have you noticed that? It's not good for his face muscles—he's going to age very young, especially if he doesn't stay out of the sun. Although the camera does love him. He's an easy sell for viewers.

You know who is much harder to film? Jordan. He was always moving and jumping around with book excitement. He's all elbows and guffaws. Bethany is in literary love with him though—she kept looking at him while she was doing her interview. He didn't really look at her, he was so focused on all his books.

TWO: The number of questions I have for you. I might be a slow reader, but Battle of the Books is soon, right? How are all those people going to read ten books? You've already read them, right? Like, twice? Isn't it going to be hard for them to catch up? (Oops, that's five questions.)

ONE: Number of people who mentioned the video to me. Like remembered I was a part of it. Not a big deal, but it seemed like everyone mentioned the video to you.

OK, I need to go over my lines for LARP Club. See? I read tons!
Piper

Grateful: Easy math, moving up in the LARP world, your warm donuts, cold donuts, ALL DONUTS

To: loveanddeceptionfan@gmail.com

Subject: BoB Meeting

Piper,

I'm writing this at night since I can barely find time to write you. Things have been so crazy. As you witnessed today at the meeting.

I'm so glad you got all those interviews on camera! I didn't even hardly notice you recording around us because I was so busy with crowd control. Those warm donuts nearly caused an earthquake because of the stampede. Come on, people. Warm or not, they're just donuts.

And then no one was really listening when Miss del Rosario was describing each book, even getting weepy during her *Old Yeller* spiel (with spoilers! Ugh). It's totally worth the read though. Jordan agrees with me. And now that I think about it, he was the only one I had a conversation with about A BOOK. Everyone else came up to me and rambled on and on about how awesome the video was and how awesome the donuts are.

Then Miss del Rosario started to quiet us down so she could give instructions. And frankly, I was a little shocked.

I pulled out my sharpened pencil. "Are we going to do a pretest?"

She tilted her head. "Pretest?"

"My elementary school teachers always gave us a short pretest before making the groups so they could see who was stronger in certain categories. Strategic team formation is vital to winning at district."

She laughed. "No, no, silly. I'm going to let everyone pick their own teams. I want the students to have ownership of the process and have fun."

I blinked several times. "Fun?"

She nodded. "Of course. That's what Battle of the Books is about!"

This made no sense. This wasn't called "Fun of the

Books." Miss del Rosario had been in the battle—at this very middle school—a long, long time ago. I had even seen the trophy her team won—it's on display in the main hall. Surely she knew that *beating* Laguna was what Battle of the Books was about. They don't use the word "battle" for no reason.

Suddenly people were grouping up in teams. It was all happening so quickly I couldn't keep up with it—like I was in the middle of a storm that was whirling around me. Bethany took control and pulled together her "dream team," which consisted of Tess, Eve, and Jordan (no shock there). But then she marched up to me. "If you're not on a team yet, you could be our alternate."

It took everything in me not to turn and run out of there. But then there was a tap on my shoulder. "There's still room on our team." It was Jackson.

Butterflies!

I grinned. "Um . . . there's . . . you . . . uh . . ." It was embarrassing. So glad you didn't get that on camera.

(You didn't, right?!)

Jackson pointed to a table in the far corner. There sat my team. Ian Speloni—Library Lurker—along with Raj and Ana Shah, the twins. "They all live on my street," Jackson said. "We ride the same bus so we can talk on the way home."

Wow. So practical. I really, really wished I lived on that street.

"I'd love to be on your team!" I probably said it with far too much excitement in my voice. But hey, it was a sentence and it was formed and it got the job done. It's so weird that I was able to have that long fifteen-minute conversation with him so easily when I was busy concentrating on a golf ball. Maybe I should keep my nose in a book so I can talk to him nonstop.

At the end of the meeting, I noticed a few students checking out some of the books Miss del Rosario shared. So I quickly did the math.

If there are ten books to read in thirteen days, that's 0.769 books per day that they need to read. If they get their homework done and don't log on to a computer, they would have 6.9 hours of reading time each night. Though they'd have to eat their dinner while reading and go to the bathroom only in emergencies (and preferably with a book in hand).

The only way I can get large chunks of work done is if I make a timetable and schedule my breaks. So my plan is to create a schedule for everyone and bring it to our next meeting. Ms. Benson is always saying things like, "Be the heroine of your own life, not the victim!"

So this heroine intends to take charge and get this group ready for a book battle. But more importantly, pull together a dream team of students to go to district.

The strange thing was that all of Miss del Rosario's reasoning for having us pick our own teams didn't seem ridiculous to me anymore. We had plenty of people joining the battle. And I—Olivia Weston—was on a team with Jackson. All due to a sweet little shoulder tap. Swoon.

So for right now, I'm going to try to stay glass-half-full, like Ms. Benson always tells me to do, and look on the positive side of things.

People attended.

People smiled.

And I'm on Jackson's team!

Speaking of teams, I wonder what schools go to the middle-school district competition? We certainly wouldn't want to use similar school colors on our T-shirts.

Hold on . . . I'll check.

Um.

Something weird is going on. Let me Google again and see if there's some mistake.

Ummmm . . . no mistake. When I Googled Battle of the Books for our area, a video popped up. Ours. Which makes sense. But it wasn't on your YouTube channel. It was on someone else's channel. And guess who?!

ZOE ALFANO!!! She's like the most famous fifteen-year-old YouTuber who ever existed! I watch all her makeup and fashion advice. I don't follow a lot of it, obviously, because she's so bold (orange lipstick! Crazy). But she's so funny and she has like a gabillion followers.

I clicked on the link, and guess what darling-famous YouTuber Zoe was talking about? ME! And you, technically! She saw the link on Juan Verde's Twitter page, because Zoe's also an aspiring actress and really wants to star in one of his books-made-into-a-movie someday.

So she talked about the video—OUR VIDEO—and said it was the best thing she'd seen on YouTube in a week! And she even said it made her want to go out and read a book and there was a link at the bottom for her followers to go watch it.

I didn't click it. I can't. This is all so nerve-racking and unusual and freaky and other words that express Extreme Emotion!!

Deep calming breath, deep calming breath.

I'm going to distract my mind by finishing my homework. And then I'm going to distract my mind some more by writing up a schedule for everyone to follow to help them read the books. Creating schedules calms me down.

So for now, no freaking out about the video and all the emotions related to it. I'm shutting my internet door and getting some work done.

See you tomorrow, director!

O

Gratefuls:

1. Zoe Alfano for introducing me to the joys of vanilla-scented hand lotion
2. Zoe Alfano for linking to our video!
3. Jordan, for talking to me about books without even side-glancing at the donuts
4. Mom's blackberry cobbler "made just like her mama made it"
5. A mom who still uses phrases like "y'all" and "Mama" and bakes cobblers, even though we're in California, where people say "dude" and eat avocados nonstop

Olivia,

Did you just tell me who Zoe Alfano is? Olivia, I was the first one to *show* you a Zoe Alfano video. I started following her when she only had two thousand subscribers. Now she has almost one million.

Going to watch the video. Please listen to this relaxing jazz music while you wait.

Zoe gushed. She gushed! And her comments section features some of the following reviews:

Yourmamaeatsburritos: What a great way to promote literacy in a fun way!

HungerGamesIsLife: This girl makes a lousy Katniss. *(So not true, Olivia.)*

PhotoKitten: Whoever made this video is awesome. I would totally watch more of her videos.

Almost a million people just saw my video!!!!!!! If she posts it directly on hers, we don't get as many views. But the link got us . . . hold on . . .

Olivia. We are up to 550,000 views.

Our video is more viral than yellow fever! (Is that a viral infection or bacterial? Or neither.) Scratch that metaphor. It has more views than that video of a baby kitten wearing a mustache. Or the one with a mustached baby sneezing on a kitten! (Man, I love that one.)

We'll talk about this tonight. I'm so glad Mom is letting you come to Talin's birthday dinner! See you in a bit . . .

Piper

Sorry we have to write back and forth. The parents go bonkers if we talk during Dad's long birthday monologue he gives every year about how grown-up Talin is now. He has used the word "proud" like twelve times.

Welcome to my life.

Oh my gosh, your brother just ate an entire bowl of chips in two minutes.

He's so gross.

But cute.

Don't call my brother cute, unless you're going to marry him so we can be sisters.

I gave Jackson Whittaker warm donuts today. I'm pretty sure I'm already betrothed.

Do you see that water drop on the paper? It's one solitary tear. I am so proud.

But should I have joined Bethany's team?

No way. This will be such a great film now! The meaningful glances across the table. Bethany looking at Jordan, Jordan pining after you...

Um, and everyone liking books, right?

Mmmm this salsa is good. Oh my gosh. Don't look now. Mrs. Nelson is coming over.

Who?

She goes to our church. She knows everything about everyone. She's staring at you.

OLIVIA WESTON IS THE MOST FAMOUS PERSON IN DON PEDRO'S!

I can't believe she recognized me. I'm so embarrassed.

That guy at the other table recognizes you too. Look, he's staring.

Piper, everyone is staring.

DO NOT tell my family that I was a part of you know what.

This is the perfect opportunity.

My mom just got me a tutor! If she knows how much time I spent on that video instead of my grades, I will have to get ten tutors.

But they could talk about it on the Christmas card.

No. My parents might get mad. And I'll be banned from video-making, probably forever.

But Talin already told me she liked the video!

Put this paper in your purse. Now!

Why did you just act so weird?

I didn't.

Yes you did. Is this because you did that video with Olivia and she's famous now?

NO. And why are writing to me instead of listening to Dad tell stories about you?

He's talking about my baby stories now. This could take all night.

Agreed. Wait ... how do you know I did that video with Olivia?

Um, because you do everything together. And it's totally your sense of humor. And I watch all your YouTube videos.

You do?

Duh. I'm your sister. So why haven't you told Mom and Dad?

I don't know. Don't tell them.

If I don't, someone will.

I'm just the director. People don't pay attention to the person making the video, just the star.

Right. So next time Olivia gets recognized, they'll ask why and someone will mention the video.

Okay. I'll tell them. In a bit.

Why wouldn't you? It's hilarious. Is this because they deleted all those files on the computer?

WHAT FILES?

Oh. I thought Mom told you. They were uploading a new calendar program and I think they deleted some of your stuff. Sorry.

Then yes. That is why I don't want them to know. Promise you won't tell.

Fine. Give me some of your fajitas.

You always eat the shrimp.

Of course I do. LOVE YOU, SIS.

From: loveanddeceptionfan@gmail.com

To: westonfamily706@yahoo.com

Subject: Eeeek! Not mouse related, Danny related!

Olivia,

Hey, sorry we haven't talked since Talin's party a couple nights ago. I have to tell you something. So we interrupt our regular session of sisterly bonding, famous people (you!), and large viewer number freak-outs (795,690) to bring you this:

Tonight. Babysitting Andrea. It started off normal. So normal I didn't ask her if you know who was around. Andrea's parents had a doctor dinner to go to. Danny's dad is a physician's assistant. I think he does different things than a nurse but didn't go to school as long as a doctor? Either way, he is the guy everyone in the neighborhood calls when they have a medical question. And they are always going to fund-raisers or fancy dinners.

So they kissed Andrea good night, gave me fifteen dollars to order a pizza, and said they would be home by eleven and that Danny was out with friends. They made it sound like he would be out with friends all night.

So I got out my babysitting bag and started to play UNO with Andrea while we ate some dried blueberries my mom bought at Costco. Then Andrea wanted to play Barbies. Of course, "play Barbies" meant reenacting a scene from that book I'm reading, *I'd Tell You I Love You, but Then I'd Have to Kill You.* I'm on page 102 and it's getting really, really good. Usually, I can spot a plot twist from a million miles away, but the author keeps me on my toes. Andrea is reading a book called *Clementine*, so I let her direct a scene. Not as action-packed as our soap-opera role-playing, but fun to mix things up.

The doorbell rang during a quietly emotional scene—we threw water on our dolls' faces so it looked like they were crying. I grabbed the money to pay the pizza guy. Only it wasn't just the pizza guy at the door. Danny was there too! He waved as a friend's parent drove off.

"Want me to help with this pizza?" he asked.

It was only eight o'clock. Andrea would go to bed at nine. His parents wouldn't be home for another three hours after. Was I supposed to leave or stay?

"I got it." I paid the pizza guy and then we were alone on the doorstep. It was awkward but not awkward, if you know what I mean.

"Yeah, I was at the skate park with my friends," Danny said. "And I was going to stay, but it was kind of windy and . . . yeah, they'd already had dinner and I was hungry, so . . . that's cool that you ordered a pizza already. My parents really wanted me to sit tonight, so I should have stayed out."

"So . . . do you want me to go home?" I asked.

"No, no. I didn't want to cut into your babysitting time at all. Like, you're here already. You should get paid the whole time they are gone. Maybe . . . maybe we'll just tell them I was out late? And then I'm just going to go to my room. To chill."

I adjusted the hot pizza so it wouldn't burn my hands.

"But . . . you want some pizza, right?"

"Yeah. I mean, if there's enough. Just a slice."

But he didn't eat a slice, Olivia. He ate three. I only ate two slices in case his parents thought I ate the whole pizza.

He did go to his room, though. So I played an episode . . . I mean, Barbie game of *Love and Deception* with Andrea and tucked her in. Danny's music was blasting the whole time. Andrea was asleep by nine. I just kind of sat there, twiddling my thumbs, not knowing what to do. It felt *so weird* that Danny Moss was in the house just . . . there. Like his parents shouldn't pay me just to have us both sitting there. So then . . . then I did something maybe kind of stupid.

I knocked on his door.

Danny peeked his head out. His music was all screamy and angry. "Yeah?"

"Hey. So . . . maybe I should just walk home? Because your parents aren't going to be home for two hours, and it seems silly to have us both in the house like . . . watching her. All she's doing is sleeping anyway. And watching someone sleep would be creepy."

"That reminds me of this horror movie I saw once." He leaned on his doorway.

I could see a little bit into his bedroom. His bed was unmade and he had posters of skateboarders and basketball players. I didn't see any dirty clothes. Or underwear. That would be so gross.

"There was this mom who loved her kids like crazy," he said. "Like almost too much. And so she would watch them sleep every night, and never sleep herself. So one time, her kids turned into zombies, like right before her eyes, and then she started trying to find a knife because, you know, zombies . . . but she turned around and realized she was dreaming and she almost cut her kids."

"That's nothing. In *Love and Deception*, there was a zombie epidemic. Randall Menard was actually such a charming and diabolical zombie, no one even noticed he'd transformed for three episodes. Then they gave him brain surgery and he was healed."

"Cool." Danny folded his arms. "Look, you should probably stay. Like I said, I don't want my parents to know I got home early. We could watch that zombie mom movie? Or another one . . . it has an old lady who likes to steal kids' toes while they're sleeping."

"Why would she do that?" I asked.

He shrugged. "I can't remember. Let's watch it."

So we did. It was a dumb movie. There were zombies in that one too. I kind of fell asleep during part of it. We didn't sit by each other or anything if you're wondering. It was like watching a movie with my brother Luke. But . . . not like that.

When it was over, I told Danny about all the cool things going on with our video. And how many views we have.

His eyebrows shot up. "Have you included ads?"

"No!" I said. "I changed the settings so I can't. No one wants to watch commercials."

"Then how are you going to monetize all those views?"

I didn't know what he meant, so I just shrugged.

"You have a window of opportunity here. How are you going to follow this and keep the momentum going?"

"Um . . . I've been filming some stuff at the meetings. I think there's a story there."

"Great. Your viewers are going to want more in that same world. But you need to do it soon."

"I know."

He shook his head. "You're, like, really talented."

"I know," I said again, but this time my face went red. I looked up *monetize* when I got home. It means make money. Of course, Mr. Owns His Own Lemonade Business at Ten is thinking of the financial angle. Maybe I should too? I don't know.

It's so many big things at once.
I'm still tingling. All over.
And I like it.

PIPER

Grateful: Meatball pizza, zombies, babysitting, making money to watch (or not watch) a kid sleep, chapter twelve of that book I'm reading. For fun. Still.

Piper,

Okay. I think we need to add some people to our valentine friend list . . .

SORTA FRIENDS

Those people in the restaurant who recognized me—would that be weird?

Zoe Alfano—maybe she has a fan mail site

FRIEND FRIENDS

The guy in the Vons produce department—without his guidance, we would not have the world's most luscious blackberries for Mom's cobbler

Talin—how cool is it that she watches all your videos and didn't say anything to your parents? I've never had a sister, but I think we should hang out with Talin more. When she's home. Which is never.

MORE THAN FRIENDS

Danny Moss

So, why did I add Danny to the "more than friends" category? Let's unpack this.

First, you hated him. Hated his hair. Hated the way he talked. Hated how he confidently skated around your neighborhood. Remember how you used to refer to him as "Danny . . . Danny who?"

But then you did a favor for him by telling Tessa he liked her. Except you ended up with a bloody nose because the two of them got into an argument in LEGO Club.

Classy.

He apologized and ended up coming to your birthday. You didn't even mind it, if I remember correctly. And now Danny-Danny-Who hung out with you in his living room and watched a movie. On a Friday night. I'm fairly certain that means you're engaged and our double wedding will happen sooner than you thought. Or maybe it just means that you guys don't hate each other anymore and everything is different now which just confirms our hypothesis that boys are confuuuuuuuuuuusing.

It sounds like a good kind of confusing.

Whatever the reason, the fact that Danny willingly wanted to watch a movie with you is suspiciously suspicious.

You need to stay on the case and investigate this boy like you're a news reporter. Find out how the male mind works. Record some data. Put it in a chart. Add some glitter. We could sell the information and make millions. It's better than our idea last summer to start a Kickstarter campaign to fund our need to help little turtles that are flipped over on their backs, which really needs to be done in Hawaii so please help us pay for our trip. It was fun thinking about Maui for a good ten minutes though.

Okay, so I know one thing for sure: Valentine's Day is in a couple of weeks and things are going to get interesting. I'm glad we already have our friends and more-than-friends list for Valentine's Day. Oh! Could we add Juan Verde?

In related news: Have you found out if we're supposed to bring cards for our class on Valentine's Day? I'm not sure what sixth graders do. We need a manual.

I'll see you at the meeting for Battle of the Books. Miss del Rosario said she plans to hold a mock battle to help us practice for the real school competition. I hope my team has been reading! My guess is you'll get some great dramatic footage.

Love,

Olivia

Gratefuls:

Sorry, no time. Gotta keep reading!!

O—

Call Vicki Lance at 800-234-1775.

She's an editor at *Little Miss Magazine*.

An EDITOR, Olivia! How exciting!

Love,

Mom

Piper.

PIPER!!!

This note was sitting on the kitchen counter. I cannot believe an actual editor found me and CALLED ME. Being an editor for a magazine or a book publisher is my dreeeeeam job (besides being a senator). I have no idea what they do, but it sounds so glamorous and I'd get to have lunches in New York City and wear chunky glasses and put all my spelling skills to good use.

I took three deep breaths, then dialed her number. (Seven. I took seven breaths.) Piper, she was the nicest person-who-is-a-stranger-and-also-an-editor that I've ever talked to! She asked me all sorts of questions about why I decided to make the Battle of the Books video and how I came up with all the crazy ideas for the book characters and where in the world did I get that adorable Laura Ingalls Wilder bonnet? I explained that I dressed up as LIW once for Halloween. (Twice, actually.)

So get this! She is featuring it on the *Little Miss* magazine website.

TODAY!

I will check it later after school to see how it turned out. Or maybe Miss del Rosario will let me check it on her computer during lunch? I mentioned her a couple of times so I'm sure she'll want to read it and pass it along to Principal Dawn.

Oh gosh, maybe Principal Dawn will be so impressed that she'll take a meeting with us. (Remember, we are important people now. We *take* meetings—we don't have them. That's Big Deal language. I think.) We might finally have the clout to convince her to make some changes to the Hallway Initiative. All that walking in an orderly manner is really cutting down on my goofing-around-with-you time.

So, if you get a chance today, stop by the library and look up the interview. I think I did a really great job. And now I'm *this* much closer to getting a job in publishing someday.

We have another battle meeting today during lunch. I really hope some people went home last night and started reading. I'm sure they did. How could they not?

Girl who chatted with AN EDITOR FROM NEW YORK CITY,

Olivia

Gratefuls:

1. That note from Mom. She was so excited!
2. Editors! From! New York!
3. Being asked questions and feeling like a little adult
4. Not choking while answering those questions
5. Our Valentine's list that keeps growing :)

From: dawn@kms.edu

To: [all parents]

Subject: Great news!

Dear parents,

Good morning! I wanted to send out a quick email updating you about the Hallway Initiative. It is off to a great start, but please remind your child not to congregate near the water fountain, since we're having a problem with this turning into a spontaneous water fight. Slippery halls are dangerous, and here at Kennedy Middle School . . . safety is first!

In other news, we've had a terrific turnout for Battle of the Books. One of our students was even featured in a *Little Miss* magazine article. Congrats, Olivia Weston! Thanks for making Kennedy Middle School look so great!

Principal Dawn

P.S. No pizza today; sorry for the inconvenience.

Piper,

This day.

I don't know what to say. It went from flying high in a hot-air balloon overlooking the Pacific Ocean to drowning in a sewer.

I'm not sure if that made sense.

Anyway.

At lunch I went to the library and Miss del Rosario already had the *Little Miss* article pulled up on her computer. She was gnawing on her nails while swaying as she read it out loud.

MIDDLE SCHOOLER SAVES HER SCHOOL'S BATTLE OF THE BOOKS PROGRAM WITH LITERARY ARROWS TO THE HEART

That was the title of the article! And then it went on to explain how I'd set such a great example for girls everywhere and they even put up a picture of me. It was my school photo from last year, the one where I look really uncomfortable, like I have a splinter in my thumb.

But then did you see the comments? So many people were talking about how awesome I am for saving the program and how Laura Ingalls Wilder would be proud of me! I won't lie . . . I totally started to cry.

It was such an amazing moment, Piper. I only wish you'd been there with me to read it. All I got was Miss del Rosario clobbering me with hugs.

So that was the flying high in a hot-air balloon portion of the day.

The sewer part? It happened at the meeting.

Miss del Rosario gave directions. "Settle down. Let's get started!"

It took a lot of shushing on my part and some stern looks to get everyone quiet.

"Each question will be worth three points if you give the correct title, and two points if you state the author's name. A total of five points."

There were some murmurs. Mostly about the maple bars that Bethany brought. Everyone on my team was listening except for Jackson. He wasn't there. Did he forget? Or did he change his mind?

Miss del Rosario asked our teams to select a captain. Fortunately, Raj, Ana, and Library Lurker gave me a look, like I was the obvious choice. Which was nice.

But all the other teams sort of fell apart giggling and playing rock/paper/scissors to appoint someone. Finally, they stopped their giggle-fest long enough for Miss del Rosario to ask the first question.

"In what book is a character punished by having to dig holes at Camp Green Lake?"

Seriously, that is so easy! But most of the teams looked like Miss del Rosario had just asked them to come up with a solution for world peace.

Then Bethany's team answered the next question. And my team answered the third one. The other six other teams were treating this like recess. Two boys started tossing a Nerf ball to each other!

Miss del Rosario clapped her hands together to get their attention. "You know what? Let's try something different. Stand up. We're going to play a game."

I hesitated. A mock competition was all I wanted to do. This wasn't a time for *games*.

She wrote all the authors' names on the board. Each team had to recite the authors' names while hopping on one foot. If they put a foot down they had to start over. Hop! Hop! Hop! Next thing you know, teams were falling over laughing and even Miss del Rosario was bent over, giggling so hard that her eyes started watering.

IT WAS A DISASTER.

It just baffles me why they would sign up and then happily walk in the door and expect it to be social hour with snacks and live entertainment. Books, people. It's about BOOKS. My only goal is to put together a strong enough team that we can get to district and beat Laguna.

To do that, they need to understand the following:

It will be hard work.

It will take many hours.

It will be more important than video games.

Or the internet.

Or watching TV. (Who even does that anymore?)

Or even jumping on one foot.

The thing is, we have a couple of decent teams so far. Mine and Bethany's. Although I'm a little worried about Bethany because she keeps following you around, hoping you'll record another interview of her since it could be her "big break!"

I kept looking your way to get your attention, hoping you'd help me fix this. Why didn't you even look my way during the meeting? I tried to hurry down the hall to catch up with you after, but you'd already hauled it off to class.

I would've kept running to catch up with you, but Miss

del Rosario called me back to read all the additional comments on the *Little Miss* article.

She's so proud of what we did.

I'm proud of what we did, too. I just wish it would turn out the way I thought it would. With people reading . . . and loving it. And then, of course, competing the way they're supposed to. This could all turn into one huge embarrassment. We can't go to the district competition with no answers and faces full of donuts.

I guess the only bright spot was when Jordan walked by me and whispered, "Your bookworm is showing."

That guy's pretty funny.

But that won't win us a competition against Laguna.

And where in the world was Jackson? Part of me wants to call him up and say harsh words, but the other part of me is wanting to be super kind/understanding/irresistible. Next week is our school competition. And the following day is Valentine's Day. What if Jackson and I worked together—in a totally romantic fashion—to win the school competition? And then what if the following day, he handed over—in a totally romantic fashion—the world's most romantic Valentine's card? It would all be so romantic. And cinematic, of course. He must be on my team to stage this super cute moment.

Except. Hold up.

What if he doesn't give me a Valentine's card? What if I get a card from someone else? Or worse . . . no one.

I have such a love/hate relationship with February 14th. It's the best and worst holiday all wrapped together in one.

Needless to say, I've been Googling "do middle schoolers give each other valentines?" I know we've made a master list of people to give cards to, but now that we're in sixth grade, I have no idea if people give cards. Our teacher hasn't said a word about "making sure you give one to every person in the class and here's a class list with names that you can give to your parents so they can help."

Do we buy the store-bought kind with superheroes? Do we still attach lollipops? Who am I even supposed to ask? Hopefully Bethany will address this in her blog. I'm too embarrassed to ask her.

Oh! Maybe I'll send her an anonymous email. If I sign it *Your Biggest Fan*, I'm sure she'll talk about it on the blog. The girl lives for fans.

I should ask Blinkie. Maybe a blinking cat can unlock all these mysteries.

I just tried calling you but you're not home.

Sigh,

Līv

Gratefuls:

1. Valentine's Day
2. Valentine's Day candy
3. Valentine's Day cards
4. Valentine's Day cards from boys
5. The Valentine's Day manual for middle schoolers that you will surely find for me!

Piper,

Okay. I tried calling you again and you didn't answer. So here is the rest of what happened. Before I went home today, I stopped by Ms. Benson's office.

"They're not reading the books," I explained. "They're laughing and playing games and it's turning into a disaster."

Ms. Benson sighed. "You're worried."

"Of course."

"What if you just let them do a bad job at the competition?"

"Why would I do that? No, no, no—I'm not going along with all that 'let them fail and they'll learn from their experience.' This is important and it needs to get done the right way. And the competition is super close to Valentine's Day and I still have no idea if sixth graders give cards and lollipops and whether I should be bold and tell Jackson I like him!" Whoa, I can't believe I said that out loud.

She tilted her head. "Sounds like you're a little overwhelmed."

"You got that right!" At this point I was stress-pacing.

She pulled out some slips of paper. "I want you to write down every worry you have. Then you're going to put them in this jar. Don't let them ramble around in your head tonight. Let them sit in this jar until tomorrow."

I filled out nine slips of paper and stuffed them in the jar.

"Thanks," I said. "I feel better."

But honestly, I didn't.

I wanted to talk.

To YOU.

I just called your house again. You're not home.

Where are you?

Respond! Please!

Olivia

Olivia,

I shot the following footage at the mock meeting. You've been so busy with fancy interviews, but I thought you should know what I captured . . .

Start with a shot of the school from outside, go through door, stop outside door where sign says THE BATTLE HAS BEGUN. Two guys dressed like gladiators are protecting the door. Thank you, LARP, for the borrowed costume!

Inside the classroom, kids are broken into different groups. They give glaring looks to the other teams. Then, cut to:

DANA HUFFINGTON, perched on a bean bag in the reading corner (*Giggles)*

Oh my gosh. There are so. Many. Cuties. Here!

Shots of different boys in room. Barry Dotter is picking his nose.

DIRECTOR

So who is your favorite book character?

DANA HUFFINGTON

I don't know. I haven't read any of the books. Well, I saw

the *Hunger Games* movie. And the *Holes* movie. Does pilgrim girl have a movie?

DIRECTOR

She's a homesteader. And there's a whole TV show for *Little House on the Prairie.*

DANA

Oh good. I'll watch an episode. Anyway, who knew all the adorable boys were kicking it in the library this whole time?

DIRECTOR

The world's best-kept secret.

Meanwhile, the camera pans the room. We catch you with your head down, skimming through a book. Jordan breezes by and bends down close, behind your left ear. Even from across the room, your face reddens. He says something, then smiles. You watch as he walks back over to his group, then glance at the camera, embarrassed.

DANA

Do they have a reading club I can join after Battle of the Books? Or a movie club! Just something that gets this many boys in one place would be super great.

DIRECTOR

(Sarcastically) Maybe you should start that club.

DANA

You are sooooo smart.

JORDAN

(After BoB, standing in front of the lockers) This is really cool that you did this, Piper.

DIRECTOR

Thanks. But remember? Pretend I'm not here. When you're talking to the camera, you're talking to the viewer, not me.

JORDAN

OK. I'll start again.

(Smiles at camera. He has a sort of self-conscious smile, but it's not bad.)

I'm really glad Piper Jorgensen made that YouTube video. It was smart and funny and appealed to a new audience. Most of these kids wouldn't be here without her idea. And Olivia's acting like she's excited about the video, but I can tell she doesn't like the attention all that much.

DIRECTOR

(Mumbling) Wanna bet?

JORDAN

(Shrugs) Look, even if these kids only read one Battle of the Book, or heck, half of a book, that's a lot more than they would read otherwise. So whether we win this or not, I'm just excited more kids are reading. These books are so awesome. It's really cool.

Olivia,

In season six of *Love and Deception*, Ann Rasher stole Taylor Lommel's husband by convincing him to leave his family for a life spent traveling the world and taking a ridiculous amount of selfies. Of course, dark magic was involved. (She then went on to get so much plastic surgery that some viewers said she looked too much like Barbie, making the whole plotline very cliché. The writers later dyed her hair red and made her temporarily go blind from staring at herself too long in the mirror. Ahh, irony.) What Ann did was horrible, but the bad dye job and vanity blindness (clinical term) was so karmic, the viewer was satisfied.

If a viewer were watching our friendship right now, I think they would see what you clearly do not. Betrayal. Of course, it's nothing diabolical like stealing a husband. I know you would never do anything that horrible. But Olivia . . . you kind of stole my spotlight.

And I really, really need that spotlight.

Laura Ingalls Wilder was *my idea*. All the characters were.

I even looked up those plot summaries you talked about so I could know enough about the books to cast characters. IN THE SCRIPT I WROTE. You didn't even want to *do* the video, remember? I had to talk you into it by using all that books-are-the-most-important-thing-in-the-world coaching. And now you're being featured in *Little Miss* magazine as the girl saving girlkind, and it didn't occur to you to mention my involvement?

Look, I know actors usually get all the credit. But in their Oscar acceptance speeches (um . . . magazine articles), they list all the people who got them there. And you give Miss del Rosario this huge shout-out, and this is all I get?

Interviewer: What gave you the inspiration for the video?
Olivia: Well, my friend. She's brilliant. Really, the whole thing was pretty much—
Interviewer: Fabulous? We totally agree.

cricket *cricket*

How about: my friend Piper did the whole thing. Script, director, producer . . . costumes!

Did you read the script from the last meeting? JORDAN GOLDBERG totally gave me credit. We weren't even talking about me and he recognized how much I've done. Jordan Goldberg, Olivia.

Look, I don't want this to be this whole thing between us. I needed some time to cool off, and I took it. I forgive you. Just next time . . . try to mention me more (or at all). It would mean more YouTube hits on my channel. I want to keep those views coming so when I post my next video, I have a big viewership.

We're at 919,023 views right now, which is amazing. I just want to make sure people are searching for videos made by me, and not videos starring you. No offense. It's just that . . . for you, this is really only about getting a couple of kids to read some assigned books, right? For me . . . this could be my whole future. My big chance. My turn to shine.

Next year, my parents can do a whole Christmas card just about this video! I mean, as soon as I tell them about it. Which might be soon. Soonish. Maybe after I get really good grades so I can hit them with a double whammy of amazing.

Talin brought it up again today while we were brushing our teeth in the bathroom.

Talin: Your video keeps getting views.

Me: I know.

Talin: Luke knows about the video.

Me: *(spitting out my toothpaste)* You told him?

Talin: No, he mentioned it to me yesterday. Said Olivia is pretty cool. He doesn't know you did it too.

Me: Oh. Okay then. Good. I guess.

But Olivia . . . I was really bothered that my sister would instantly figure out that I was a part of the video but Luke wouldn't even put two and two together. I mean, *obviously* I did the video. It's what I do. But maybe he doesn't even remember what I do. Maybe if Talin had told him, he would just shrug and give a lukewarm reaction (sorry about the pun).

I know this is super weird. I'm mad at you for not giving me credit. I want it. I want all the likes and follows and views. But at the same time, I'm worried it's a bottomless pit, like it won't ever be enough. Especially if my parents don't care.

Which is so weird, because I've never cared about any of it before that stupid Christmas card. Or maybe I didn't realize I cared until now?

So yeah, maybe I overreacted. I don't know. Sorry?

This is too emotional. Moving on . . .

Battle of the Books. Remember, it takes other people way longer to read a book than it does you. So I wouldn't worry so much if the rest of the participants weren't as into it as you. You only need a couple of people to care enough to make your team. Do you really want everyone reading if they aren't on your team? That's competition, right? This is probably better for you. You've done your duty and gotten more people involved. Sit back now and enjoy the ride. (The ride that I started driving. Mention Me.)

Actually, I picked up *Holes* in between filming. It just like . . . jumps right into things. I like that. It's almost as good as *I'd Tell You I Love You, but Then I'd Have to Kill You.* I'm on chapter fifteen. Cammie just told her friend Macey this huge secret and . . . you know. I won't spoil it for you.

Also, what's with you saying that I should add Danny Moss to my More Than Friends list? The guy isn't an absolute jerk all the time. But that doesn't get him to soap-star status.

Also, I feel like this book stuff is taking over your brain. Leave all your worries in Ms. Benson's worry jar and enjoy this.

Pipes

Interviewer: What gave you the inspiration for the video?

Olivia: Well, my friend. She's brilliant. Really, the whole thing was pretty much—

Interviewer: Fabulous? We totally agree.

Piper, I did mention you.
They cut it. You wouldn't even let me say something at dinner with your family.
You are sending me mixed signals.

Hi, Mrs. Jorgensen! May I text with Piper for a moment?

Of course, Olivia. You have such great manners.

Thank you, ma'am.

Hey.

Hey.

Did you just "ma'am" my mom?

I AM half Southern. Biologically.

Okay.

Sooooooo.

I'm sorry.

I talked about you with the reporter. I really did!

Silently?

I was ambushed! I'm so sorry the parts about you weren't included. That New York editor was asking questions so quickly. I wasn't even sure what to say.

How about: let me give you Piper's number. Can you interview her too?

You could've said something like that.

But sometimes I would start a sentence and she would finish it for me. Like she was in a rush! Is that what happens to people who live in New York City?

You were able to finish your sentences with Miss del Rosario's name.

She kept leading me to talk about her. And she kept mentioning deadlines and this being a "hot story" right now.

Yep. It is. It's YOUR hot story.

I thought about calling you—I really did—but you haven't even told your parents about all this. What would happen if I called your house and your parents found out that you were taking calls from a fancy New York City editor?

They'd probably call the police. And get me three more tutors.

Exactly. So why won't you just talk to them about it? What's the worst that could happen?

Look! Squirrel! Did that take your attention to something else?

Piper.

I'm erasing all these texts from my mom's phone. I don't want to talk about it right now. Next topic.

Fine. Will you come to the school competition? It's on Friday.

Are you going to attempt a conversation with Jackson? Not that it would make good drama for the video, but . . .

Of course it would. That is, if he shows up. But then again, I have no idea what to talk about. During math class I asked him if he liked HOLES.

And?

He said yes. He loves donut holes.

No. He didn't.

Yeah, he did. The guy thinks this whole competition is about pastries.

At least Jordan seems to get the point.

He does. Totally.

You should call him and ask to study together.

Hello?

Liv?

That just gave me butterflies. WHY DID I JUST GET BUTTERFLIES WHEN I THOUGHT ABOUT JORDAN??!!

Stop it.

Oh good grief. If you start using the happy face wearing the pilgrim hat, I will end this.

See you at the competition.

I'm going to wear my "The Battle Has Begun" T-shirt. Let's be twins.

Twins.

Always. MENTION ME!

I'm printing your name on a banner. Promise.

$$\frac{2}{5} \times \frac{5}{4} = \qquad \frac{7}{8} \times \frac{6}{3} = \qquad \frac{10}{5} \times \frac{1}{2} =$$

$$\frac{9}{7} \times \frac{2}{6} = \qquad \frac{10}{9} \times \frac{3}{5} = \qquad \frac{2}{3} \times \frac{4}{2} =$$

Jackson, why weren't you at the mock battle? We could have used your help. Even though we never had time to do a mock battle due to everyone having a good time and laughing hysterically.

SORRY. OUR TEACHER MADE ME REDO A FRACTIONS QUIZ THAT I BOMBED. ARE WE REALLY GOING TO USE FRACTIONS IN REAL LIFE?

Three-fourths of me wants to scream, "Of course!" But one-fourth of me thinks fractions are rude for causing you to miss the meeting. See you at the competition?

SURE. NOT SURE I'LL BE MUCH HELP. NINE-TENTHS OF ME KNOWS THAT YOU'LL DO GREAT. THE OTHER THREE-TENTHS OF ME IS JUST LOOKING FORWARD TO THE SNACKS.

The math on that was . . . a little off. But I'm a fan of snacks, so please come!

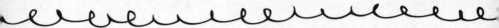

Piper,

The previous note happened in math class today. Please note
that I am the one who initiated this exchange of words. I really
need to look over my Valentine's Day card to him. It needs to
be the right blend of wit, humor, and utter perfection.

Help,
Olivia

From: loveanddeceptionfan@gmail.com

To: westonfamily706@yahoo.com

Subject: Pod People Out of Pizza

Olivia,

We need to start a new list. It goes beyond More Than Friends.

GUYS WHO ARE OBSESSED WITH OLIVIA

Jackson! Jordan! Anyone with a J name!

I have zero experience with this, Liv. I don't think this is a love triangle. Maybe a Like V? Who says you can't like both of them a little for different reasons? It's not like you need to choose between them. Tomorrow, you might start crushing on the Library Lurker too. Pretty sure there are no limits on crushes. I presently am in deep like with three brothers. They're characters on a TV show, but still. Roll with it. Besides, I'm enjoying all this Intrigue! Drama! Scandal!

Tonight, my family went to Pizza Palace for the buffet. Talin received the Distinguished Scholastic Athlete award from some tech business, which also meant a $2,000 college scholarship. She also gets a trip to San Francisco to eat expensive cheese in some museum with other Amazing Kids.

I'm super excited for her, not that she needs my excitement. The pizza place gave her a free cookie pizza. They don't do that for just anyone.

Anyway, here's tonight's dinner conversation.

"Luke. Not too many breadsticks," Dad said while he helped himself to a third serving of cheesy bread. "Protein protein protein."

Luke sighed. "But we're at pizza and pasta paradise. What do you want me to do, eat a stack of pepperoni?"

"Pepperoni!" Flynn said. "Pepperoni!" (That kid loves some pepperoni.)

"So, Piper." Mom bit into a slice of meat-lover's pizza. We are a pro–processed meat family. "Tell me about your tutor. Did you discuss your curriculum goals? Does she seem like she can cover all the subject areas effectively? Were you polite?"

"Which question do you want me to answer first, Mom?" I asked.

"When did you get a tutor?" Talin asked, genuinely

confused. To be honest, I think Talin is sometimes confused when I talk at all. She's very pretty, and I think sometimes pretty people see other people in varying degrees of visible. To her, I'm half ghost.

"I started tutoring today," I said. "We don't need to talk about it."

"No, tell us," Luke said. "I've never had a tutor. Does she, um, do homework with you or something?"

Or something. Olivia. She had me do THREE HOURS of evaluation tests on the computer. Each test was fifteen minutes long, and it covered every topic imaginable. After the third test, she let me stretch and eat two Skittles. Not two packets of Skittles, just an orange and a green Skittle that she set out on the kitchen counter. What am I, a mouse?

Her name is Mrs. Bey. Her hair is red and white and brown. She wears it in long, clunky braids. Also, she wears fruity perfume and track pants. And she cracks her knuckles a lot. "She's nice. Yes, I was polite." I rolled my eyes at my mom. "I don't know what we are going to learn yet. I think she's just figuring out what I know."

"No comprende?" Spencer asked. That's right. My toddler brother knows more Spanish than I do. I patted his head and fed him more peaches.

"Well, that's cool," Talin said. "Are any of your friends in tutoring with you?"

I laughed. "It's not a club. We aren't playing flashcard games and giving each other high fives. My grades stink and I have to do it."

"Pipe, we don't talk like that around the twins," Dad said.

"Stink!" Flynn and Spencer said in unison.

"Well, er . . . that's cool, Pipe," Luke said. "Maybe you'll end up liking it."

I ate some more salad. It wasn't really salad so much as blue cheese dressing with a tiny bit of lettuce. I was crunching a crouton when the thought came to me . . . just tell them—tell my family about the video. Why not? If they don't care, they don't care.

I just made that sound so easy. But suddenly the crouton caught in my throat. I wanted them to care. I wanted to go to dinner to celebrate things that I had done too. I wanted them to be nice to me because they thought something was cool, not because they felt bad that I had to do tutoring.

I wanted to be equal in the Christmas card picture and letter. I wanted to be more than JUST Piper.

I swallowed. "So, hey. Kind of a crazy thing happened."

"Are you sure I can't eat some pizza?" Luke asked Dad. "Or a ravioli?"

"Protein calories are better for building muscle," Dad said.

"Mom, can we buy me a new dress for my scholarship ceremony?" Talin asked.

Mom beamed. "And shoes."

No me gusta!" Spencer said. (This means "I don't like." I think. Isn't it great that I'm learning Spanish through my toddler brother? Isn't it annoying at the same time?)

"Guys. Listen. I was at Battle of the Books. At school—"

"Oh yeah. I did that," Luke said. "Our team went to district, but I had a basketball tournament and missed it."

"Well, Piper joined!" Mom exclaimed. "It's very scholastic of her. I'm sure it will help improve her schoolwork."

"That's the thing, Mom," I said. "I didn't exactly join. I'm kind of a . . . witness. Like, I oversee the, uh, characters."

"Like the captain?" Luke asked.

Talin shook her head at me. Like you would. "That's not what she's saying, Luke."

Dad ruffled my hair. "See? That tutor is helping already!" So, how would a tutor I met just a few hours ago help something I had done a month before that? This is the truth about my family: they are all aliens. Or pod people. Or cardboard cutouts designed to look like people related to me. Because we can have the same conversation at the same time, and yet it is actually two conversations happening on separate planets.

"Hey, I saw your friend in that video, Pipes," Luke said.

Mom smiled. "What video?"

"Online." Luke grinned. "It's something else. I'll show you later."

Is "something else" good or bad?

And then my throat closed up. I couldn't do it. Not after all this tutor talk and Luke going to district. I wanted to have a moment like I did in the library when our video premiered. I wanted a moment like Talin was getting, with everyone beaming and excited and no one asking her if she did her chores and homework before she won an award.

"Ay, caramba!" Spencer said.

Luke and my parents laughed. Talin tugged on my sleeve.

"Come on. Tell them."

"I'm getting more garlic bread," I said.

"Get me some!" Luke called out.

"Son. PROTEIN," I heard Dad say. Then they started talking about nutrition again.

I loaded my plate with cinnamon pull-aparts.
How could I explain that my involvement with Battle of the Books has nothing to do with books? Or even how a video getting likes matters when there isn't a fancy cheese reception attached to that honor? What if I did tell them, and then everyone was disappointed, like the thing I'm *finally* good at is not the thing they want me to be good at?
It's so weird that the people I live with and who I spend every day with have no clue that this major event is happening in my life. We might as well all be living in an apartment building on different floors, smelling one another's cooking and maybe glancing in an open window by accident, but only knowing one another's last names because they're on the building mailbox.

Except for Talin. She wrote me this note tonight and left it on my bed:

What in-the-sisterly-kindness happened there? Maybe I'm
not totally invisible to Talin. Or maybe she feels bad for me. I
can't tell.

I'm going to go edit some more of the footage I got. I might
need a second cameraman to get candid shots while I'm doing
interviews. I'll make sure to get all the live shots tomorrow
though for the school competition. Remember everything Ms.
Benson has ever taught you about anything.

Breathe. Wear a color that makes you feel courageous. And I
know you don't totally get this concept but—have FUN.
Piper

Grateful: Pull-apart bread, Spanish, TALIN, keeping my
secret a little longer, soooo many views

From: westonfamily706@yahoo.com

To: loveanddeceptionfan@gmail.com

Subject: Re: Pod People Out of Pizza

Piper,

You tried. But sometimes—and no offense—your family can be overwhelming. Everyone talking at once. Everyone having different opinions. Toddlers already knowing a foreign language.

Just don't give up on the whole "truth" thing. Okay? Like Ms. Benson says, things may work out better than you ever imagined.

Except right now, I don't think I can take that advice for myself.

Dad was running late for dinner so Mom announced, "Throw on a cute sweater. We're heading to the Cheesecake Factory!"

I had no idea which sweater to pick since the lighting in that restaurant is so decadent. Gold tones. Soft up-lighting. It's Mom's go-to spot when Dad's not nearby.

White. I chose a white sweater and Mom actually seemed impressed. She even rushed back upstairs to change to her own white sweater, so we could match.

As we glanced over the menu, I couldn't keep my eyes off their Glamburgers. But Mom—being Mom—couldn't even wait until we'd ordered until she started in. Remember, she has a PhD in prying, so this wasn't shocking.

"Honey, if you don't mind me saying . . . you've been awfully busy lately. Is the Battle of the Books competition making your schedule this packed? I mean, you are as busy as a one-armed paper-hanger!"

Oh, Southerners.

"Yes, this is about the competition." I flipped to the back and eyed desserts. Something about knowing a chocolate mousse cheesecake was headed my way at the end of my meal made me excited. And talkative. The mood lighting also probably helped. "Mom, I don't know how to say this but . . . I'm not excited. I've been squishing my stress ball far too much. The whole thing has been a bit of a mess."

She shook her head. "Messes are not good." Mom is particular about things that are out of place, physically and emotionally.

"No one is reading the books. They're just having fun. And eating donuts. I mean, thanks for the Krispy Kremes. They were a hit. Maybe too much of a hit."

"Warm Krispy Kremes will motivate anyone."

"Not this group. And Miss del Rosario didn't even make the teams according to ability. Glamburger, extra well, and a Sprite." The server had walked up. Mom ordered a Cobb salad since it was Grandma's specialty.

Mom folded her napkin and leaned in. "Sorry for the interruption. Go on."

Her listening skills were sometimes as good as her asking skills.

"Remember last year when our teacher made a board game with all the questions and we practiced every Friday—the whole entire class did? After we took that pretest, she figured out the top two teams, we battled, and bing-bam-boom, DONE. Off to district . . ."

"Mmmm-hmmm." She couldn't really talk because the server had dropped off a plate of bread and butter.

"This year's competition has been one huge mountain of drama. Which is good for Piper's documentary, I know, but it's not good for my nerves." I paused and then added in a soft voice, "You *know* me, Mom. I'm not the girl who likes to be in the spotlight. I'm just . . . me."

Mom grabbed my hand and squeezed it. "You got this, sugar."

That hand squeeze, her calling me "sugar" . . . it made me feel better. The burger and cheesecake made me feel better too.

But as I sit here on my bed thinking about tomorrow, I can't help but worry about having to step it up and answer a lot of questions if I'm going to have a chance of going to district. And I have a feeling I won't.

Ugh. There I go again with my catastrophic thinking, just like Ms. Benson always says.

Blinkie tells me I'm being totally catastrophic right now.
(That's what he is saying when he quickly blinks twice and
then one long blink.)

So, I'm sure my team pulled through and studied like crazy
tonight. I emailed them some sample questions but I haven't
heard back from them yet. They're probably busy studying.
It'll be okay.

At least you'll be there documenting it all the way.
See you soon, bestie,
O

Gratefuls:
1. Cheesecake
2. Glamburgers
3. Bread & butter
4. The second round of bread & butter our server
   brought to us
5. A mom who likes to wear matching sweaters to dinner

Welcome to
KENNEDY MIDDLE SCHOOL'S
Battle of the Books
COMPETITION

Watch as
we narrow down our
large field of students
to just **ONE** team.

They will go on to the
district battle next week!

So step inside
if you love **literature!**

Also . . . shhhhh. This is still the library.

From: dawn@kms.edu

To: [all parents]

Subject: And the winners are . . .

Parents,

Today we held our annual school Battle of the Books. It was a festive event and the students had a great time watching the teams battle it out. Congratulations to Olivia Westcott, Raj & Ana Shah, Jackson Whittaker, and Ian Speloni for making it to the district battle! We hope some of you can come and support our team.

In other news, the students are doing great with the Hallway Initiative and there are far fewer injuries reported. Also, we are aware of the strange smell coming from the boys' locker room and we are working on finding the source. Please make sure your child is washing PE clothes at least once a week.

In related news, we have scheduled an adolescent hygiene assembly.

Principal Dawn

Piper,

Do not let Principal Dawn's letter fool you. When she says "festive," I believe what she means is "FIASCO."

According to my thesaurus, *fiasco* also means "a breakdown."

"Failure."

"Flop."

"Botched situation."

"Dumb thing to do."

(Swear, this last one wasn't made up by me. IT'S ACTUALLY IN THE THESAURUS.)

The library was so chaotic—all the team members dashed around to find their spots. Then we had to quickly decide on an alternate. Miss del Rosario said we should wait to pick an alternate until just before the competition since we wouldn't know who was sick until that morning. Something told me Jackson might just be the one who was sick.

I emailed him last night to double-check if he'd received

my previous emails with sample questions. Yes, you're reading that right. I emailed the boy and didn't even die doing it.

But whatever, he never wrote me back.

I scanned the library, looking for his perfectly gelled brown hair. But all I saw was floppy brown hair . . . Jordan's hair. He waved wildly at me from across the room. I waved back, to be polite. I wasn't sure why he'd want to be friendly with anyone on the enemy team. I was his biggest competition, and yet there he was . . . happily . . . waving.

Jackson showed up at the last minute. He rushed over to me.

"I was worried you might not come," I said.

He looked a little pale. "I volunteer as alternate." This *Hunger Games* reference was pretty adorable. But then after noticing the look on his face, I realized he didn't even know he'd made a cute reference.

"We can decide as a team," I said.

He stuffed his hands in his pocket. "Last night, I tried to read as much as I could. But with homework taking me hours, all the words started to jumble together. I'm not sure I remember any of it."

It hit me that he probably didn't want to tell me all the details about how hard homework is for him. I didn't need to make him feel any worse.

Also, I wonder if I will ever be able to breathe normally

around him. Or if my heart will ever stop slamming in my chest when he's close. When adults are in love, do they feel like this all the time? And if so, who wants to be in love anyway?

There was a voice behind me. "I'll be the alternate." It was Ian Speloni/Library Lurker/Boy Who Shockingly Just Spoke Four Words.

Jackson shook his head. "Naw, man. I will."

"It's okay. I'll do it. You play."

"No."

"Yes."

"No."

"Yes."

It went on and on like this for a couple of weeks.

"Please—" I interrupted. "The competition starts soon. Can we decide—"

Library Lurker shook Jackson's hand. "Good luck. If you need a replacement, I'll be in the back row should anyone throw up or get abducted by aliens."

Poof! He disappeared.

My guess is Library Lurker doesn't like to compete with books, just read them. But he does seem like an okay guy. I'll refer to him by his real name from now on. It's the right thing to do. Well done, Ian Speloni—nothin' but respect.

So, the competition. Here are the highlights of what could

only be called a FIASCO (told with bullet points because I love anything dot-shaped).

- Someone, probably Bethany, had organized a volunteer team of students to bring in baked goodies and fill up the back table. How do I know it was Bethany?

- The tablecloths were our school colors and sprinkled with glitter.

- Bethany is the obvious suspect. I am not dumb.

- The audience chatted, snacked, and waved at your camera.

- We huddled. As captain, it was time for me to give some sort of heartfelt speech and cheer them on to a Big Win. This moment was supposed to be inspiring. Cinematic!

- But they were so distracted; it was like they weren't even listening. Raj and Ana started bickering over which one of them had checked out a book longer than they should have. Since they're twins, they borrow a book and share it. Unfortunately, it sounded like "sharing" didn't happen and they weren't familiar with all the books, just a few. So I turned to Jackson. But before I could give him a pep talk, he'd run off to the snack table.

- Just before the first round began, Jackson returned with armfuls of sugar-in-the-form-of-donuts.

- I ate two. Just to be nice.

- I might give up donuts after this is all over. Yes, I said it.

- Across the room, I saw Jordan cheering his team on. He asked them something, not sure what, and all I could hear was them yelling, "Donuts!" And then Jordan shook his head and looked as frustrated as I was. It kind of made me feel like I wasn't alone.

- He also ate two donuts.

- The battle began with Principal Dawn reminding us about the hallway rules. Then we finally got to the good part . . . the battle rules!

- "I will ask each team a question about the plot of a novel," Miss del Rosario explained. "You must answer with the title of the book and the author's name. In that order. With fairly decent pronunciation."

- My team was up first.

- Bring.

- It.

- On.

- "In which book does a character have to dig holes in a dried-up lake bed?"

- So easy. I didn't even look at my teammates for help. "*Holes*, by Louis Sachar." I had looked up the pronunciation of the author's name. The "ch" is actually a "k" sound.

- Jordan's team was next. He nailed the question about *Out of My Mind*.

- But then the next fourteen minutes blurred into a jumbled mess like the entire event had just been thrown into a blender at Jamba Juice.

- Bethany's team was far too busy scarfing down a plate of Oreo brownies and even Bethany herself was far too busy trying to get YOUR attention to even answer Miss del Rosario's question. I guess she wanted to have her every moment recorded for her fans.

- It was nice to look out in the audience and see Ellie waving at me, cheering me on. But you were busy trying to get away from whatever that Becca girl was doing in the audience. There was a lot of shouting cheers and standing and sitting.

- What in the world happened?!

- Bethany stalled and giggled, stalled and giggled, never coming up with an answer to the question. How did she not know the answer was *Little House on the Prairie* when Miss del Rosario even used the word "prairie" in her question?! She's done Battle of the Books for as long as I have, so I know she could have gotten the answer right—she was just too busy having FUN.

- I REPEAT, THIS IS NOT CALLED "FUN OF THE BOOKS."

- *Breathe, Olivia, breathe.*

- It took both Miss del Rosario and Principal Dawn a few minutes to get everyone settled down and forbid them from eating any more snacks until the competition was over.

- Competition.

- Ha.

- And this concludes your bullet-point storytelling moment.

Needless to say, my team won. I answered almost every question without even looking to my team for answers. Sometimes you gotta do what you gotta do.

Afterward, Raj and Ana charged up to me. "Why didn't you let us help out?" Ana asked.

"You guys admitted that you didn't get to read all the books. I had to make sure we won if our school ever has a chance at taking on Laguna." Then I realized I was sounding a little rude. Okay, very rude. "Look, there's time before the final battle to study some more. It will be more of a team effort."

They smiled. Sort of.

Jackson left and headed to his next class without even saying, "Thanks for winning the competition," or, "Good job," or, "Expect the most romantic valentine from me tomorrow."

Maybe Jackson *should* be the alternate at district. We may have a better chance at winning and it's possible Jackson will have to come congratulate me due to school loyalty and/or romantic feelings. Ohmygosh, what if he hugged me? Gosh, even a handshake would put me on the map.

But honestly, the part that hurt the most today was watching Bethany and everyone else follow your camera around hoping to get in your "rad vid." Yep, your videos have a street name now.

It's like they didn't show up for the right reasons. This is about memorizing characters' names.

Plot.

Motivation.

Setting.

Correct pronunciation of the author's name.

I never intended this to turn into some pop-culture reality show! Maybe you shouldn't film anymore. Everyone is too anxious to get on camera and they don't even care about the reading.

Winning at the district competition is all I'm focused on.

And honestly, I'm not sure it's going to go my way.

Why did I even start this to begin with?

I mean . . . I won the school competition. And I'm not even happy about it.

This was never what I wanted to feel.

Olivia

Olivia,

I think you're right. Mostly. I'm not sure this turned into what you wanted it to be. Or what I wanted it to be. Yes, there was Drama! Intrigue! Scandal! But it was fake. And just generally a mess.

So beforehand, when the groups were paired off, I thought I'd get some cool shots of everyone huddled up. I wanted to hear inspirational speeches and heartfelt cheers. But instead, people would see me coming and stare into the camera. YOU NEVER STARE INTO THE CAMERA WHEN DOING CANDID SHOTS. And then they would smile, or giggle and say, "Look, it's Piper. We're on camera." The audio ended up being muffled. And when Jordan was trying to rally his troops, he asked, "Why are we here?"

Everyone cheered, "Donuts!"

"No, guys. Because we love books!"

Which I think Jordan meant. But no one else was buying it.

Then we all got on the stage, and Principal Dawn got up and thanked everyone for following the Hallway Initiative.

Oh, and loving books. I mean, every movie has some guru or fountain of wisdom motivating the warriors, but she just kept talking about gum being banned because people were sticking it on their lockers. Where was the inspirational speech? Something that would get the audience to clap and cheer?

Then . . . oh, Olivia. When a question got asked and no one knew the answer and the audience was bored and the kids on the stage were bored . . . there was just this heavy, awkward air in the room. I could Auto-Tune, add music/animation/whatever, and nothing was going to save the sinking ship.

Then . . . Becca! She tried to start the wave in the audience. And when that didn't fly, she loudly whispered, "Hey. Piper. Get this!" And then she stood up, pumped her fist, and started chanting, "The battle has begun! The battle has begun!"

I mean, to twist my words to suit her own commercial purpose . . . it was just wrong. I didn't film her. Halfway through, I just shut off my camera. I couldn't make a story out of dead space.

Doing that YouTube video was so fun. Even if a million people hadn't watched it, it was still so fun. Creatively. And this . . . it felt like a chore. And it's not like anyone cares if I really make another video. We wanted more people to join the battle, and they did. So I guess we accomplished our mission? Danny asked me how I was going to follow this up and . . . I don't know. The footage I have now doesn't equal my previous work. And I don't know if I can really move forward in this field if my family doesn't know.

I started writing a letter to my parents, telling them about the video. I've written five drafts so far. I would add them here, but they've already been burned.

My job is to film my siblings' accomplishments. My job is to babysit the twins. My job, in my family, is to stay in the shadows. I know you hate the spotlight, but at least you have some choice in the matter.

So today I told my mom I had the Battle of the Books competition, which is the truth; I just didn't tell her that I wasn't *in* Battle of the Books. She told me she would pick me up after school at the flagpole.

Danny was sitting out there with this kid Hampton. Remember, we used to call him Hamper in first grade? Anyway, I sort of kept my distance, but then Hamper left and Danny scooted over to me. I don't really know if I was in the mood to talk to him or not. I felt, like, emotional already anyway, although I couldn't pinpoint what emotion I was feeling. I didn't want to add in whatever feeling/emotion came from talking to Danny. I just wanted to go home and finish the last three chapters of *I'd Tell You I Love You, but Then I'd Have to Kill You*. (There's a plot twist coming! I can sniff it.)

"Hey, Piper. You get any good footage?" he asked.

"No." I shoved my camera into my backpack. "It's hopeless. No story to tell."

"Add zombies." Danny grinned. "Anytime a story gets boring, just make a zombie pop out. Or make zombies come out of the books."

I halfway smiled. It wasn't that bad of an idea. "So there's zombie Katniss?"

"And zombie Charlotte! Spiders are already creepy."

"Where were you an hour ago when everyone was trying to grab my camera so I could make them famous?"

"Oh yeah, by the way, I'm just talking to you for the famous thing," he said. "You know that, right? Do you think you can get me on *Shark Tank*?"

I punched his arm. Which was maybe, like, playful. But whatever.

Then my mom pulled up and leaned out the window. "Piper. Hurry. Your tutor is going to be at the house in ten minutes."

I don't know where my mom came from or what she was thinking. In what galaxy is it okay to mention my *tutor*? In front of a kid my age. Who is a boy. Named Danny.

I grabbed my bag. "See ya."

Danny stood up and waved at my mom. "I had a tutor.

Last year. Helped my grades so much."

I paused. "Really?"

"Yeah. It's not a big deal."

"Okay."

"Piper!" Mom called. Has she forgotten what it's like to be twelve?

"Uh . . . thanks, Danny." I ran over to the car.

I didn't know what I was really thanking him for. But all the bubbling emotions weren't so bubbly anymore. I didn't even say anything to my mom for yelling "tutor" out loud. I didn't even say anything to my mom at all. She asked how Battle of the Books went, and I said okay, which wasn't a lie.

Maybe we need to go to Cheesecake Factory together like you did with your mom. Maybe some Snickers cheesecake will help me open up?

Then I went home and did homework with the tutor for a long hour and a half. But at least when we were done, I understood things more and knew I had the right answers on homework. I should probably start figuring out another career path now that it's clear this movie thing is a bust.

Honestly, why did I think the documentary was a good idea? Should I bag this whole filmmaker thing? I loved getting all those views on YouTube, but what if nothing I ever did succeeded again? What if I never succeed? Will my parents be, like, embarrassed by me?

Am I going to be "Piper . . . just Piper" for the rest of my life?

I'm sorry everyone likes donuts over books. Maybe pour maple glaze on all the pages before district? Then we can make signs that say, "You'll devour this book."

Also, we'll add zombies.

Love,

Piper

GRATEFUL: Snickers, snickerdoodles, short car rides, having three more chapters to read!, DANNY HAD A TUTOR

C⊙MET

EXP... ...ORE. PAY LESS:

CA sales tax: 8.00% Cashier: Alex

STATIONERY-OFFICE

1	Star Wars valentine pack (jumbo)	$4.99
1	My Little Pony valentine pack	$1.99
1	Blank valentine pack (generic)	$0.99

GROCERY

| 1 | Oreos | $3.99 |

4 ITEMS

SUBTOTAL	$11.96
TAX	$0.96
TOTAL	$12.92

| CASH | $20.00 |
| CHANGE | $7.08 |

Olivia,

The most recent episode of *Love and Deception* actually had a fresh spin on Valentine's Day. Tatiana Vickers is in an insane asylum, again, because she suffers a severe phobia of phobias (also known as phobophobia). While she is in the insane asylum (do insane asylums still exist, or aren't they just regular hospitals now?), we meet additional characters who suffer from the following phobias . . .

1. Xocolatophobia: fear of chocolate
2. Philematophobia: fear of kissing
3. Anthophobia: fear of flowers
4. Cardiophobia: fear of hearts
5. Amoraphobia: fear of love

So, of course, the whole place goes bananas on Valentine's Day, because each of their phobias come out. There is a fire, and one of the patients hides in a pond until they remember they have limnophobia, fear of . . . well, ponds. Also, McKay Davis dresses like Cupid and still somehow manages to look dignified and attractive. Such is his way.

My point, Olivia, is this is the year you finally got over your TalkingtoJacksonPhobia. Don't forget how far you've come. And maybe the best way to seal the deal is through a card. Maybe this will smooth everything over after BoB. Remember when I wrote that note for you to give to him? Then you ended up writing your own note, which you accidentally gave to Jordan, who now also likes you.

Decide what you want Jackson to be to you and make it very clear in the card. The timing couldn't be any more perfect. If you give him a card that says L-O-V-E on the front, it's clear you like him. If it's something like "Let's BEE friends!" then he is in the friend zone. If you give him one with kittens in a basket, you are soul mates. Btw, Mom bought tons of Valentine's cards that were on sale at Target. I'll hand you a stash.

What *do* you want Jackson to be, by the way? Because the Olivia that I used to know would do anything to get an opportunity like this to have Jackson around more, even if he didn't like books. The old Olivia would DEF give Jackson the extra-large Star Wars valentine with TWO suckers attached.

(I think the same rules from elementary school valentines still apply.)

(I think.)

I wonder if Cammie ever gives Josh a valentine? Maybe, since she is a spy, it's written in invisible ink? I'll let you know if that's in the next book. Almost done with the first one, and I think there's a sequel.

Yesterday, during lunch, I went to the bathroom so I could finish reading the chapter I was on. Which was pretty weird, and probably gross, since it's a library book and you have to wonder how many people read in the bathroom, if you know what I mean.

But *I'd Tell You I Love You, but Then I'd Have to Kill You* is so good. *So* good. I won't spoil it for you, but please read this book soon so we can discuss.

Oh, I just had a great idea for valentines and Battle of the Books. I'll text you on my mom's phone about it soon. As you can imagine, Doodlebug is cray-cray busy right now, so I'm watching the twins all weekend and editing my video.

Also, happy Valentine's Day early, BFF!! I'm including a little valentine I made you.

Love you (unless you have a phobia of best friends).

(I'm sure that's called BFFOBIA.)

Piper

GRATEFUL: Target, a useful website that explains phobias, candy, the secret meaning of two suckers, books (well, this book. Not allll books)

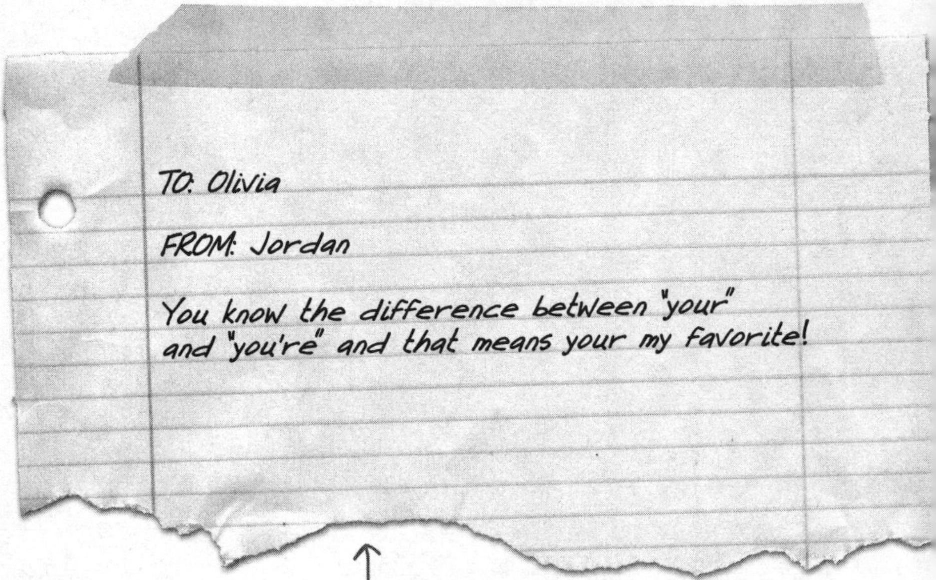
TO: Olivia

FROM: Jordan

You know the difference between "your" and "you're" and that means your my favorite!

Jordan slipped this inside my locker. That last "your" is misused so I laughed due to me being a nerd. I couldn't help but wonder if he'd given a valentine to any other girl . . .

Um . . . no. Read on, friend . . .

★ BETHANY'S BUSINESS ❤

HOME   NEWS   EVENTS   ABOUT   CONTACT

Hey, Bethanites!

It's Sunday. So you know it's time for . . .

SUNDAY STATS!

36: Number of valentines I received

20: Number of Battle of the Books books I read
(I read them twice)

3: Number of bouquets. And only ONE was
from my dad.

0: Number of valentines I got from this boy
I like. I'm not going to say his name, but . . . I
mean, I decorated his whole locker! Would a
little card have hurt? I just hope he didn't give
anyone else a valentine. Like he doesn't celebrate the holiday because it's too commercial.
Then it's not so bad. But if someone DID get a
valentine, that would be like . . . sigh.

SHOUT-OUTS

★ Jackson Whittaker: Wow, Jackson made a valentine for every single teacher. That's just really special. Actually, any guy who takes the time to make a valentine for a girl is pretty awesome. Or not even make one . . . just write a girl's name on a premade one. Or a Post-it Note! Post-it Notes aren't asking for too much, right? Heck, I'd even take one ripped from notebook paper! (Kidding, that would be insulting.)

★ Miss del Rosario: This lady has made Battle of the Books so much bigger than it was in the past! The school competition was today and . . . I hate to break the news to you guys, but . . . my team lost. Surprising, I know. But it was like my brain was somewhere else. There was so much going on with that whole snack table I organized and then the documentary Piper was filming . . . honestly, I just wasn't having my best day. But, I'm taking the high road here (the view is so pretty from the high road . . . I learned that on a Hallmark card) and saying a big CONGRATULATIONS to Olivia and whoever else was on her team. Hopefully, we will beat Laguna! If not, that's okay because we had the best snacks today and so many laughs. This is a tradition that needs to go on forever!

CELEBRITY GOSSIP

Ever since Juan Verde tweeted about Olivia's video, our school has been on the map! If his next book is made into a blockbuster movie, it's possible they'll pick our town to film it! So who knows . . . there could be talent scouts all over town now, looking for the next big thing.

Safety note: if someone says he's a talent scout and asks you to get into his van, RUN! My mom wanted me to mention that.

WHAT'S HOT

AFFECTION!
It comes in all forms. A hug, a nice word, a VALENTINE. Goes a long way. I repeat for all you procrastinators . . . SENDING A VALENTINE WILL

GO A LONG WAY. AND PROBABLY CHANGE YOUR LIFE. (And mine, hopefully.)

DARK COLORS

Midnight blue. Deep gray. Black. It's winter, and naturally the mood is gloomy. I mean, in other places besides California. I shall be wearing all black for the rest of February. With a little pink, but that's just because it works so well with my complexion.

DRESSING LIKE YOUR FAVORITE BOOK CHARACTER

I'm sure you're all sick of hearing about Olivia's YouTube video, that has like a gazillion hits now. That said, the girl started a trend. Everyone is wearing bonnets now like Laura Ingalls Wilder or Harry Potter glasses or Katniss braids. If you aren't wearing something literary, you're totally out of style.

That's it for tonight! Need to practice hairstyles for BoB competition. It's tomorrow, you guys! Piper's been filming, and I think she's featuring me. Can we say big break?

COMMENTS:

JamieheartsScience: Dark colors?! I just donated all my gray clothes to the thrift store! I thought pastels were in. Ugh!!

Bethanyblogs: That's what you have me for, Jamie! Keep checking back regularly and you'll get all the fashion advice you need. Just throw on a gray jacket on top of your yellow sweater and you'll be stylin' in no time! And I have TONS of pink accessories you can borrow. Oh! Future business idea: jewelry rental!

Becca555: I really hope I appear in Piper's video! I did my best to call out a cheer during the middle of it so Piper would have to film it. Maybe she'll drop a beat and Auto-Tune it. It'll be hysterical!! And sorry you lost the competition, Bethany. But if it makes you feel any better, not too many people were paying attention and I'm not sure they noticed. Because: DONUTS.

DjTyler: I wore a solid-color shirt today. Do you think that will look good in Piper's video?

PalmDesertPersonalInjuryLawyer: I enjoyed your writing. If you are in need of personal consultation regarding an injury you sustained on the job, please contact us for your $200 gift certificate toward your trial fees! Call 1-800-429-OUCH.

BethanyBlogs: Bethanites, do NOT call this phone number. It's a phony. Can someone message me how to turn off all these spam comments??

Your Comments Are Welcome!

Ms. Benson—

I stopped by at lunch but you were in a meeting. I think all the great counseling skills you have aren't working on me. I'm probably the most difficult student ever. I tried to take control of my life, be positive, all that. But nothing is turning out the way I want it to. I'm sorry.
Olivia

~~Your Comments Are Welcome!~~

Olivia,
So sorry I missed you. Things will turn out okay. I promise. It isn't always the way you PLAN it to be, though. You can't always change your situation . . . only the way you REACT to it. You can choose to react happily. Some good has come from all this, I'm sure of it.

Ms. Benson

Piper,

Ms. Benson said in her note that things don't always turn out the way you planned. If she was talking about Valentine's Day, she sure was right. I never did give Jackson a valentine. I figured I'd wait until he gave me one, then I'd lay it on him. Of course, that moment never came.

But then I read Ms. Benson's note and realized I can choose to react differently. On Bethany's blog, it says that even if a valentine is given late, it still counts.

So I took a risk, and went for it.

At 8:05 this morning, I clutched the valentine I made Jackson. Double suckers on a Star Wars card. The clearest way I can think of to say, "I LIKE YOU." "WE ARE POSSIBLY SOUL MATES." "MAY THE FORCE BE WITH US."

With the card in hand, I neared his locker. But then I overheard that Dana girl and her crew laughing about two sixth graders exchanging Star Wars cards and they were using words like "lame" and "embarrassing" and "soooo third grade."

Me and third-grade memories don't like each other, so what did I do?

I shoved the card in my backpack and scuffled away in a hurry.

It was obvious that my dream of Jackson and me working together on our team and then wrapping it up with romantic valentines was not going to happen. Why does Ms. Benson keep telling me to take control and think positively when things don't work out the way I want . . . not at all? What's the point?

Anyway, there I was, the day after winning our school's Battle of the Books—a day that I should be twirling with happiness and brimming with confidence—but I was unable to slide a stupid Yoda card inside his locker.

When will I ever not be nervous around a boy?

Confused,

Olivia

Gratefuls:

Unavailable at this moment.

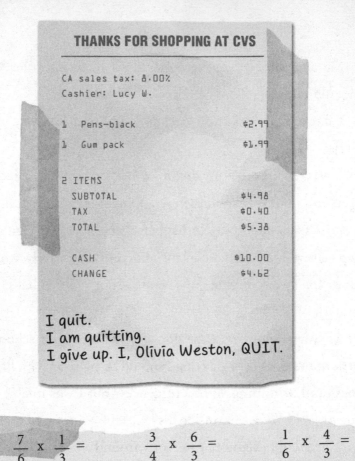

THANKS FOR SHOPPING AT CVS

CA sales tax: 8.00%
Cashier: Lucy W.

| 1 | Pens-black | $2.99 |
| 1 | Gum pack | $1.99 |

2 ITEMS
 SUBTOTAL $4.98
 TAX $0.40
 TOTAL $5.38

 CASH $10.00
 CHANGE $4.62

I quit.
I am quitting.
I give up. I, Olivia Weston, QUIT.

$$\frac{7}{6} \times \frac{1}{3} = \qquad \frac{3}{4} \times \frac{6}{3} = \qquad \frac{1}{6} \times \frac{4}{3} =$$

I give up. I quit.

You will participate in games and run around for the mock battle. One team from each school will go to the district competition! We compete with all the middle schools in our district. It's an entire day off from school! And yes, there will be pizza! Join today!

Miss del Rosario . . . I'm done. I quit.

Piper,

I had to include these. This explains why I wasn't able to talk on the phone last night. My mind was too busy trying to figure out what words to say to Miss del Rosario today.

This whole thing has turned into a circus. We had a little check-in meeting with my BoB team this morning and everyone laughed and talked about how cool your video is going to be instead of talking about the *actual* battle and they didn't even seem to be bothered that I was on the verge of tears.

Our school is going to be an embarrassment. My parents know I helped Miss del Rosario organize all this and now our school will be a laughingstock. How can I alone possibly beat Laguna? I've been reading these books since the beginning of the school year. But even *I* need help sometimes.

So that's why I wrote "I quit" on every scrap of paper I could find. To give me the confidence that I can march into Miss del Rosario's office and say it loud and proud.

Except, here's the thing, Piper. Remember in third grade when I got upset about the Savannah Swanson incident where they invited me to a party that didn't exist? And all that humiliation made me give up on making new friends . . . for years.

And then there's Badminton Club. Spelling Club. LEGO Club.

I quit ALL those. Heck, I even quit Chess Club for a few minutes one day when the team captain was driving me crazy.

Which brings me to this: I'm a quitter.

I am, Piper.

How did this happen? Why can't I enjoy something with all its ups and downs and just see it through? It seems like everyone else finds ways to laugh and enjoy themselves— sometimes for an entire day.

I don't think I will ever be that person.

After school, I'm stopping by the library to tell Miss del Rosario I quit.

This whole thing turned out to be a miserable mess. And no offense, but your video is part of the problem. If not the whole problem. They were all so focused on getting airtime and getting famous that the whole competition was a bust.

I know that your video is what got everyone to join in the first place. I know that. But somewhere along the way, we lost our sense of purpose.

I guess that all adds up to this: I'm done.

-O

Gratefuls:

    I

    Quit

    And

    That's

    Okay

(I hope it's okay. I really don't know, Piper.)

Liv,

Okay. Let's take a break from discussing Battle of the Books here for a minute. For an hour. For a day. You're having a hard time, but one thing I know about you and hard times is they don't stay hard. You'll figure it out. And there's no sense in me telling you how to figure it out, because you do it best on your own. But you know half of what you said isn't true. More than half. You *are not* a quitter. You are the most non-quitting person I've ever met. You are still way too hard on yourself. Deep breath. Wear whatever color reminds you of peace.

   Okay, look at this . . .

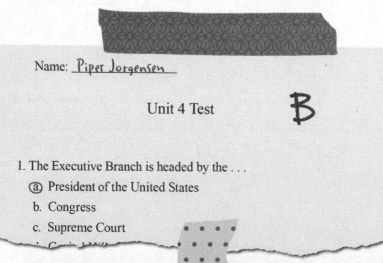

Name: Piper Jorgensen

Unit 4 Test   B

1. The Executive Branch is headed by the . . .
   a. President of the United States
   b. Congress
   c. Supreme Court

I know you get As on your tests all the time. And it's not a big deal.

I've gotten As on tests before. It's been a while, but still. This isn't the best grade I've ever earned.

But the difference, Olivia, is this time I understood what they were asking me. Because I knew the material. So I was able to read the questions and think about what I already had learned and everything made sense.

When I usually spend a lot of time guessing. Multiple choice . . . I like that better. Because it's hard to guess on an essay. And my point is . . .

The tutor is helping. And the thing she said to me that helped was, "Do you like to read at all?"

So I told her all about the Gallagher Girls series. Like . . . the whole book. Because I finished it! THE WHOLE BOOK. My mom is taking me to the store to buy the second one. There are SIX books! It's like finding out there's a lost season of *Love and Deception* out there.

"Why do you like this book?" the tutor asked.

"It reminds me of my favorite TV show. Like, it's comfortable and . . . familiar? Like I'm talking with my best friend."

"Perfect. So . . . say you're reading a chapter on the Revolutionary War. Read it like you have to explain it to your best friend, like you are the only way they can learn these amazing facts."

And I did! I thought of you, and I thought about how we would talk about the Battle of Bunker Hill and musket balls. And then that's how I sort of wrote my essay. And now that I read Gallagher Girls . . . I want you to read it. You'll love it. And we can talk about it!

Look, I'm not saying I have this deep passion for school all of a sudden. But maybe I get why you love reading a little more. When things make sense, and you can share that sense with someone else, it's more fun.

Don't forget that feeling, Liv. It's kinda part of you, in a non-cheesy sort of way.

Also, Mom put my test on the fridge and did this whole happy dance. And I decided I'm going to tell her about the video, as soon as I figure out how. Because I want my parents to be proud of me. But I want them to proud of me for the things that make me *me*. Sure, part of that is understanding my schoolwork (finally). But there are other parts, and they love me, so I should show them that. Right?

Final thoughts about the video . . . it was a good idea, Olivia. Even if things got out of hand. Even if everyone is stalking me now so I can make them a celebrity. Even if I didn't get the kind of attention I hoped for from the experience. Even if the video stops getting views and people forget about it.

I don't know if I can ever do something like it again, but . . . it is good.

And I am proud.

Piper

GRATEFUL: I read a book! I'm going to read more! I'm telling my parents about the video! I GOT A B!!!! (Also, cheese. Unrelated, but mmmmm.)

Kennedy Middle School

Olivia—

Please reconsider. I know you want to beat Laguna, but you're forgetting the best parts of the battle. We take a bus ride to the competition. Laugh. Eat snacks. And yes, we try to win.

But win or lose, it's all exciting. Being around other kids who have a love of books is like finding your home.

I found mine there . . . almost twenty years ago.

Miss del Rosario

Piper,

I wasn't sure what to think of Miss del Rosario's note. That last line about being there twenty years ago wasn't surprising. I mean, I knew that she had gone to this school because she told me that one of the Battle of the Books trophies in the main hall was from the year she attended Kennedy Middle School.

I've walked past that trophy display hundreds of times, never stopping to take a better look.

Until today.

Mom dropped me off and I shuffled inside the school, shoulders drooped, backpack sagging, head hanging . . . not the picture of a happy girl. That's probably why Jordan ran up to me.

"You okay?"

I shrugged. "Define okay."

He looked up at the sky, like he was trying to find the answers in the ceiling tiles. "*Okay* means good with the world. Not fantastic or anything, but sort of like . . . you found a surprise snickerdoodle in your lunch—smooshed but edible. That's the definition of okay. I'm pretty sure."

I slung my backpack over my droopy shoulder. "I'm not okay. But thanks for asking."

As I sauntered off like a sloth looking for a warm blanket to crawl into, Jordan caught up with me and just kept on asking me questions about my mental health.

"Today's not Monday," he said. "So you can't be having beginning-of-the-week blues. And *Doctor Who* was on last night, which I don't even know if you watch that, but if you did—believe me, there'd be a spring in your step."

Here I sighed heavily, but he was on a roll.

"It's also the birthday of my all-time favorite Brazilian soccer player. Well, actually, it's his half-birthday, so I wanted to go ahead and admit that in case you Googled it later." He cleared his throat and came to a stop, stopping me right along with him by clamping down on my shoulders. "Which brings me to the only possible remaining reason why you are walking around with a raincloud over your head. Tomorrow's the district competition for Battle of the Books. Are you worried about whether you'll beat Laguna?"

"Nope." Here I pushed my shoulders back because I needed to show some passion. And return to my normal height. "I'm not worried because I'm not going to compete."

His eyes turned into truck tires—the kind on eighteen-wheeler trucks, that's how surprised he was at those words. He didn't even ask why. Just stared.

"I feel like I'm not doing it for the same reason everyone else is doing it," I said. "They're all eating, laughing, having a good time. But I take this seriously. I'm sure Miss del Rosario did too when she was in the competition decades ago. I don't want to let her down. But I shouldn't be on that stage under the spotlight . . . I'm afraid I would hate every minute of it."

He narrowed his eyes and grinned. "Come with me."

Here he grabbed me by the arm. (My arm, Piper. It was weird and kinda cool and stop smiling, I don't want to talk about it.)

Jordan dragged me down the main hall and over to the trophy display. "Haven't you ever read the article?"

"What article?"

He poked at the glass with his finger. "The one the local newspaper wrote about Miss del Rosario . . . twenty years ago. Read it."

I leaned in closer.

Piper . . . this article . . . it was here the whole time and I never even read it.

I took a picture of it so you could read it too.

FIRST ANNUAL DISTRICT BATTLE OF THE BOOKS

The first ever Battle of the Books was held at the district office. Teams from all ten nearby schools attended as they battled it out over comprehension questions about ten books they read over the course of the year.

"The excitement for reading was contagious," said Marjorie Garnet, superintendent of schools. "We will definitely start making a tradition of this."

One student, Nikki del Rosario, who was a member from the winning school, Kennedy Middle School, shared her strategy. "We chose who would be on our teams and had fun while we practiced. We learned while laughing—that's why we won first place. But honestly, none of my teammates really seemed to care what place we came in since just participating was such a blast! A local author was one of the celebrity judges and the only thing we cared about was getting her autograph. It was all worth it for that. In fact, it makes me want to become a writer someday. Or get any job involved with books!"

Do you know what this means? Miss del Rosario used the choose-your-own-team strategy at the very first Battle of the Books. That she was *in*. Representing *our school*.

TWENTY YEARS AGO! And that experience is what led her to becoming a librarian.

So why was I quitting?

It instantly made me think of Badminton Club—the one I quit because I banged up my knee on the first day.

But, Piper, what if I had *stayed*?

Twenty years ago, going to the first Battle of the Books is what led Miss del Rosario to realize she wanted to live a life surrounded by books. What if she had quit simply because she didn't think she could win?

I don't want to miss an opportunity to discover something new about myself—maybe even what I want to do with my life—just because I was scared. Or worried it wouldn't turn out *exactly* how I wanted it to.

So here's the thing: I have decided that part of me is dead. That's right . . . DEAD.

I can't keep quitting my way through life.

I turned to Jordan and smiled. "I'm going to iron my nicest blouse and get on that bus tomorrow."

He walked me to class and didn't say another word. Just smiled the whole time.

I don't know if I'll see you there tomorrow at the district battle. But I do know this: Miss del Rosario handed you the right book—that spy book—at the perfect moment and you read it. The whole thing. So now you're a documentarian of readers and also a reader. Welcome, my friend. This is a wondrous place.

I hope you show your parents the video. I hope you decide to keep making them. It would be cool if you caught me losing and simultaneously smiling . . . and then put it up on You-Tube. Because who cares! Let's have fun. I think I'm ready to let people see that part of me, especially considering you're letting your family see the parts you are nervous to share. Even if it's a million people seeing me again, it's the ups and downs that make life such a roller coaster.

I'm going to start enjoying the ride.

Love,

Olivia

Gratefuls:
1. When a "certain boy" asks if you're okay
2. When you admit you're NOT okay instead of pretending you are
3. When you realize you can figure out a way to make things okay!

4. When you decide to enjoy the ride, and MEAN IT

5. When you make a list of gratefuls and your best friend knows that the word "you" means "me" (or "I"? I'm pronoun confused.)

O,

"I'm going to start enjoying the ride." I want to film you on your bike riding along the beach and have you voice-over that quote. What a turning point!

YOU GOT THIS.

Apparently, I got this too. *This* being the support of my family.

Because I told them.

Finally. Without throwing up!

Here's the script:

ME

(Approaches family, who are all lounging in the family room, either doing homework or playing on various electronics. I'm clutching the laptop, breathing deeply, trying to remember everything Ms. Benson ever taught you. Positivity!) Hey, everyone. So I made this video with Olivia for Battle of the Books. Wrote the script, directed, picked out costumes . . . everything. I'm proud of what I created. Here you go . . .

(Plays video. I'm pretty sure the world stopped spinning. I stopped breathing. Lots of stopping happened.)

LUKE

Hey, I've already seen this video. That's your friend Olivia. Oh, so wait . . . you filmed her?

TALIN

Duh. Piper, does your tutor ever work with people on their common sense?

LUKE

(Ignoring Talin) Dude, that is so cool. My sister is totally famous. Not you, Talin. My cooler sister.

TALIN

I'm *so* glad we can talk about this now. Because I've been thinking, do you need help marketing? Brainstorming? My friend does these nail-polish videos and they are huge. Seriously, she just paints her nails and everyone wants to watch. This is a way bigger deal though.

ME

Oh, I think this is my only one I'll post. Probably.

(And then. Finally. The reaction I was nervous about.)

DAD

(Jumps up and gives me a hug. A HUG, Olivia.) Well, you have to do more videos! This is serious talent.

MOM

(Beaming) It is so neat to see how you've grown as a film-maker! Although I love the Barbie videos you post with scenes from *Love and Deception.*

ME

You've seen those?

MOM

Of course! I follow your channel. But you haven't posted in awhile.

ME

Oh, I started a new channel. I didn't want anyone watching Olivia's video to see my other stuff.

DAD

Why not? Your other stuff is great. Like Talin said, you can use that to market yourself. Have you started working on more videos?

(I start breathing more normally at this point.)

ME

Sort of. I was doing it documentary style, but everyone just wanted me to make them famous. So there wasn't a story to really tell.

MOM

Well, what about Olivia? Is there a story there?

(And then . . . Olivia. I had just read your last letter. And the letter you got from Miss del Rosario. And I suddenly had . . . this idea.)

(PLEASE DON'T BE MAD. And please don't say no.)

ME

Actually, our librarian was in Battle of the Books when she was a kid. And she has a lot in common with Olivia. So I was thinking of showing how the battle has grown, and things have changed, but it's still about the same stuff.

MOM

(Kisses me on top of my head) Now *that's* brilliant. I'll bawl through the whole thing, I'm sure. You still have to get your homework done.

ME

I know. I got my homework done while I was going to BoB.

MOM

(Squints her eyes) So you weren't in Battle of the Books. You were filming all this?

ME

Yeah. Sorry. Don't be mad.

MOM

Why would I be mad? You're developing a talent. You're remarkable. I'm so glad you found something you love doing.

TALIN

With a million people watching! That's bonkers.

MOM

All I care about for you guys is that you find a passion and stay dedicated. And I want you to learn in school. And get good grades. And be really happy.

TALIN

(Laughs) High expectations much, Mom?

MOM

Do you really think I have high expectations?

TALIN

(Laughs harder) If expectations were a building, you'd be the Eiffel Tower! Piper babysits all the time, she does all our family videos, photography, and she still keeps up with her knitting and LARP and stuff. She's like Old Faithful in our family, and you take that for granted. Do you know she was scared to tell you about the video?

MOM

(Blinking) Were you?

ME

(Shrugging) Sort of. I didn't know if you would be mad.

MOM

But why on earth would I be mad?

LUKE

Can you introduce me to some other YouTube celebrities,
Pipe?

DAD

Well, this is great. It's not news, but it's great. Piper has
always been extraordinary.

*(Wait, what? Remarkable? Extraordinary? Old Faithful?
Why were these words coming out of my family's mouths
and how on earth were they meant for me?)*

ME

Mom. Here's . . . what bothered me. In the Christmas letter . . . all you really said is, "Piper is just . . . Piper."

TALIN

(Rolling her eyes) I told you that Christmas card was stupid, Mom! And we all had to wear plaid. Gross.

MOM

(Her face falls. She grabs my hand.) Honey, that's
because . . . I mean . . . anyone who knows you knows
how wonderful you are. Just being you . . . like Dad said,
you're extraordinary. I guess I didn't list much because
you're just my kid who has always known who she is and
what she wants. I should have said more. I'm so sorry.

ME

So I'm not the invisible middle?

DAD

(*Crushing me in a hug*) You're the jelly in this Jorgensen sandwich. Without you, our family is just a bunch of slices of bread.

SPENCER

Am I the tuna?

LUKE

Different sandwich.

FLYNN

I want jelly!

LUKE

Can we help? With the next video?

ME

You want to help? Me? With my thing?

(*My family all looks at me like I'm crazy. Maybe I am crazy. Maybe I was doing too much of that catastrophic thinking. Maybe I understand why you were scared to step out in the spotlight, but maybe I like how it feels to know my family still sees me as a star.*)

ME

Okay. But don't think I'm going to make you guys famous or anything.

DAD

(*Snorts*) You forget. I'm Mr. Brake. I have the

third-most-popular commercial at the Tuesday 1:00 a.m. time slot.

TALIN

(Flips her hair) I've never tried acting. I totally want in!

MOM

(Puts her arm around me and pulls me in tight) If you're not too embarrassed, would it be okay if I took a day off work and drove you and Olivia to the competition?

ME

(Grins; taps her on the nose) That would be more than okay. *Way* more.

So, my friend. It appears we are going in a new direction. I'm still going to use some of the footage I have of the BoB kids. You know, eating maple bars, laughing. But now I have a human interest story. And even if no one watches this video . . . I'M interested. I'm excited about creating it, with ten likes or ten million.

We got this, Olivia. Win or lose, watched or . . . ignored. We got this.

PIPER

Grateful: For my family. All seven of us.

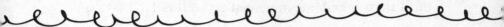

Piper,

Where are you?

You're nowhere to be found.

Our conversation on the ride here was exciting. Your idea to make this documentary have more meaning is awesome. I have a feeling it won't disappoint. And I kind of love how your mom kept leaning forward to get a glimpse of us in the rearview mirror as we talked. I'm pretty sure she wanted to be sitting in the middle of us chatting away too.

So get this . . . you won't believe where I am. Sitting in the last row of the auditorium where the district battle is going to take place in a mere ten minutes. You may be wondering why I'm sitting in the last row of the audience instead of on stage.

My team was gathered in the corner going over the questions. Even from far away, I could tell they were looking at the list of questions I had emailed them to study. They were doing it . . . studying!

Miss del Rosario patted me on the shoulder. "I tried, I really did."

I narrowed my eyes. "Tried . . . to . . . what?"

"Yesterday when you told me you were quitting, I asked your team if they'd like to also back out. I told them Bethany's team could take over. But it was unanimous . . . they wanted to go home and study. Jackson was the one who said they'd let you down."

Now I really narrowed my eyes. "You mean my team—"

"Is going to try to win this one for you."

It took everything in me to not hyperventilate. True, I'd had a moment of weakness and backed out, but how did they suddenly become so . . . amazing?

She nudged me toward my team. "They don't even know you're here."

Slowly, I approached them. I tapped Jackson on the shoulder. "Can I volunteer as alternate?"

His face lit up. Like he was excited to see me. I can't describe how that moment felt. Like fireworks and s'mores and fuzzy socks. "You're here!"

Raj threw his hands in the air. "We shared our books!"

Ana stepped in front of him. "We finally finished reading them all. I'm sorry it took us so long."

Ian pushed his hoodie off his head. "I thought you quit."

"I was going to quit, but then I changed my mind."

Jackson stuffed his hands in his pockets, his signature

move that means . . . I'm not sure. "Cool," he said. "So you can take my place."

"Actually, I changed my mind again. You guys worked hard for this. I'd love to be the alternate. You know . . . in case of alien abduction."

Standing there, watching them smile, bouncing with excitement to get on that stage made me realize that *I* was the one who made things difficult. Like the battle meetings. They weren't reading the way *I* read. But they were enjoying books, even if in a different way . . . talking about stories, watching movies, discussing their favorite characters—sheesh, even the fact that you know all the plot devices in every *Love and Deception* episode means we have so much in common.

I need to stop strangling every situation until it turns a different color and instantly becomes what I want. If I keep doing that, I'll probably be unhappy most of my life. (That should really be on a fortune cookie. Imagine how many people it would help!)

"Hands in," I said. We all put our hands on top of one another. "B-b-b book it . . . on three!"

One, two . . . "B-b-b book it!" we all yelled out, and my team took off for the stage as I headed for a seat in the last row.

I wasn't participating in Battle of the Books for the first time ever.

And I couldn't stop grinning.

Before I took my seat, I heard screeching. It was screeching in the form of a cheer. Remember how Bethany has that addiction to cheering for anything? Well, Bethany, Jordan, Tess, and Evie—our second-place team—skipped into the auditorium with balloons, a giant Kennedy Middle School banner, and matching T-shirts that said "I only battle for books."

Jordan rushed up to me. He handed me a T-shirt and a balloon. "Ready to cheer our team on?"

I was. I really was.

A warm feeling rushed around my head and I almost felt dizzy from happiness. It hit me that the phrase Ms. Benson had written in her note to me—the one that confused me like crazy . . . suddenly . . . made sense. I can't control everything; it's not possible. But I can control how I *react* to situations.

And sometimes things will turn out better than you ever imagined.

So alert the news media because I—Olivia Rose Weston— who gets straight As and knows all the presidents' names, am *finally* getting it . . . "it" meaning "happiness."

Watching Jackson up there with his team, answering questions with so much enthusiasm . . . I realized that things turned out perfectly. We didn't beat Laguna. We came in second place.

But it was awesome. Also, he is adorable.

So let's focus on the glass-half-full stuff: lots of students started reading who wouldn't have if you and I hadn't made that video. That was my goal to begin with. So what if we strayed from the path . . . we got there!

Things turned out strangely, wonderfully perfect, Piper.

And it wasn't because of me. Without you, this wouldn't have happened. I'm sorry if I ever made you feel unimportant. Piper-being-just-Piper is a beautiful thing.

All your pushing, prodding, and cheering made me come out of my shell and step into the spotlight. Thank you, friend.

But I'm still not sure where you are . . .

Piper?

Piper?

PIPER'S IMPROVED DOCUMENTARY

Show fast-motion shots of kids joking around, giving high fives, flipping through books. Show students walking through hallway of the school, teams setting up, tables being set up.

Old-timey banner across the screen:
  Battle of the Books! Where readers fight for literacy!

Show shots of Miss del Rosario. She's sitting on a picnic bench and there's a redbrick wall behind her. She has on one of my mustard scarves, because the lady is into this whole wears-lots-of-red-black-white thing, and this video needs more zap!

MISS DEL ROSARIO
Do I talk to the camera or look at you?

ME
Whatever makes you feel more comfortable.

MISS DEL ROSARIO
(Scratches at neck, then begins) How I feel about books is how my uncle Rick feels about barbecue. He totally loves it. And when you really love something, you want to share. Sure, he could sit around munching his award-winning brisket by himself all day. Ooh, and ribs. I

love his ribs. But part of the fun is seeing someone else discover something you know will bring them . . . this might sound excessive . . . but joy.

During the end of Miss del Rosario's monologue, thumb through pages and pages of books, stacking them into a tower on her desk.

Shot of Olivia. She's sitting in a leather wingback chair. She has on a frilly lace top, but it's not grandma-ish. Also, her hair is down and in loose curls, because I like when she does her hair that way, and sometimes she's too devoted to headbands.

OLIVIA
(Rubs her hand against skirt) Is this going to be fast, Piper? I really want to get back in there and cheer on my team with Jordan.

FILMMAKER (me, obvs):
He can feel your support from here. Bethany also brought the entire cheerleading squad to cheer with him, so I think it's okay.

OLIVIA
(Glances at door) Oh, do you think he likes a cheerleader?

ME

I think he likes books. I think you like books. *(Edited out: and you probably like each other.)* So let's stay focused. What did you get out of Battle of the Books?

OLIVIA

(Shrugs) It was fun. I love reading, and it was fun to see your video do so well.

ME

An answer like that is not going to win me documentary of the year, Liv.

OLIVIA

Well, I guess . . . I thought this needed to be about books. Books books books. Books all the time. I thought everyone should appreciate them exactly the way I do. But this is also about friendship. And sharing ideas. And yeah, donuts. I don't know a lot about sports, except for football. Go Bulldogs! But I do know that you can be the best athlete in the world and be on a team and not win. Or be an awful athlete and win a Super Series.

ME

Um, the Super Bowl. Or the World Series.

OLIVIA

Yes. Either of those. I haven't been on a lot of teams.
Chess Club is awesome, but it's still you against the
opponent, one on one. So I had to learn how to do this
working-together thing. Even if that meant quitting.
And . . . it was a good feeling. So . . . did that answer
your question?

ME

I'll edit it so that you did. Now. Talk about Miss del
Rosario. What did you learn from her?

OLIVIA

Miss del Rosario used to be an eleven-year-old girl who
loved books the same way I do. We probably read some
of the same books and had some of the same thoughts
and feelings while reading the same words. And of
course, totally different thoughts and feelings, because
when you read a book . . . you own part of that story.
So even though we memorize events and themes and
characters, that piece of owning . . . it's still there.

*Then do acoustic voice-over music for the end. Show the
winners being announced and everyone cheering and
clapping. SLOW FADE . . . End with a book on the stage,
and last light going out.*

*On-screen: The battle is over. But the journey . . . has
just begun.*

Piper,

That. Was. Amazing.

Miss del Rosario just finished showing your documentary on the big screen here in the library. She says she's going to keep showing it to classes throughout the day until everyone has seen what you made.

Your vision and style—it's so sophisticated. Seriously, I hope UCLA has a young documentarians program over the summer. You would get in *for sure*.

And I probably shouldn't tell you this, but there were a couple of people who wiped tears away during the video. Miss del Rosario, of course. And me, of course. And in a dramatic turn of events, guess who else wiped away a tear?

Bethany.

I overheard her talking to her crew as she blew her nose in a napkin. "I should have focused on books more. I was so worried about how I looked on camera." *Sniff, sniff, blow.* "And now it's too late and my team didn't even get to compete at district."

This cry-fest couldn't go on. I tapped her on the shoulder. "I was wrong, too," I said. "I was too wrapped up in the competition. I should've attempted to have some fun."

Which made me laugh because you—of all the people in the world—know exactly how to make any situation interesting and fun. AND YOU'RE MY BEST FRIEND. So it's probably time I follow in your footsteps. At least every once in a while. :)

After class, everyone left for lunch and Miss del Rosario let me rewind it to my favorite parts. No, I did not watch myself being interviewed. (Does my voice really sound like that??)

Now I'm going to rewind it one more time . . . oh! Wait!

Jordan just walked into the library.

BRB . . .

Okay, I'm back!

He, um.

He . . . ohmygosh I'm out of breath. Not sure exactly what just happened. You tell me:

Jordan: *(Sweeping his hair out of his eyes, sort of adorably)* Hey, Liv!

Olivia: *(Blushes, says nothing) (Notes that he called me Liv and that, too, is sort of adorable)*

Jordan: Are you watching the video again?

Olivia: Yeah. *(Not sure if that was cool to admit)* *(I need a pocket-size version of you so I can get solid advice whenever I need it. Scientists, get on that.)*

Jordan: I wish I had time to watch it with you again. My lunch break is almost over, but I wanted to see if . . . *(His voice fades away while he stuffs his hands in his pockets. He acts like he's waiting for me to finish his sentence.)*

Olivia: See if . . . there are any books in the library? *(Nailed it)*

Jordan: Uh, yeah. I could use a new book. But also . . . *(More hand stuffing, more hair sweeping)* . . . I wanted to see if you like to play putt-putt golf.

Olivia: *(Does nothing; turns to stone)*

Jordan: It wouldn't be a date or anything. It's not like I have a car. *(He laughs.)* Or money. Or nice clothes.

Olivia: *(Laughs)* *(Freaks out inside)* *(Decides to speak so he doesn't think I'm a rock)* Sure, I want to go to play golf. We could . . .

Jordan: . . . meet there? Sometime?

Olivia: *(Not even taking a moment to think about it)* Yes.

Jordan: Okay, then. See you around! *(Slinks off. Even his slinking is adorable.)*

Olivia: *(Calling out after him)* Didn't you want to get a book?

Jordan: *(Smiles)* You pick one. I'll read whatever you give me.

Olivia: . . .

Thank you again for holding; your friend will return shortly.

Piper, I'm back. I found him a copy of *The Outsiders*. I heard it's going to be on the list for Battle of the Books next year. Having him on my team will be a blast.

Also, Jackson and I are meeting in the library next week. Apparently, he's really into graphic novels and he wants me to read some of his favorites. So, um, that would be two planned interactions with two different boys.

Which brings me to this . . . I used to think Jordan and Jackson were both confusing because of their "boyness," but so much of it was just me. Me being nervous. Me being worried. Me being scared.

But I'm going to put nervous/worried/scared Olivia in a box and slide her under my bed. That analogy was sort of graphic, but it reminds me to choose the Olivia that's in the happy/confident/fun box.

That's the girl I want to be.

I bet you never saw that ever being said by me. See? Things don't always turn out the way you planned, Piper.

Sometimes they turn out much better.

In fact, last night, Dad and I went to the grocery store and no one even recognized me. It was awesome!

~O

Gratefuls:

1. A pre-grateful for you NOT asking me if I like Jordan or Jackson

2. Me, for not knowing which one I like because I don't NEED to know—not right now

3. Going out in public without being recognized— I think I'm safe now. But I know it's because everyone is obsessed with that new viral video . . . the one with cats wearing hats.

4. That spring is in the air! Can you smell the sweetness? (No, it's not leftover Valentine's candy.)

5. Speaking of spring . . . the dance is coming up. I have a feeling it's going to be all sorts of drama . . . but in the good way. :)

Kennedy Middle School

Dear families,

The Hallway Initiative has been a success! Students are moving between their classes with ease and comfort. It's downright enjoyable in the halls of Kennedy Middle School now.

But that doesn't mean we should stop being diligent about school safety. Since spring is coming, we must deal with one of the biggest dangers out there: flip-flops. You wouldn't believe the foot/toe/heel injuries that can occur from this footwear. So please step on board our NEW initiative . . .

DROP THE FLOP.

Let's be safe out there!
Principal Dawn

P.S. No hamburgers available at lunch today; sorry for the inconvenience.

Olivia,

This was on the fridge today . . .

Yes, the YouTube views are awesome. And double yes, feeling like I'm not an alien in my own family is lovely. But! I got a call from the school district asking if they can post the documentary on their website. And maybe on the CALIFORNIA STATE OF EDUCATION'S WEBSITE.

I'm feeling crazy smartsy now.

But even more important: I can't believe Jordan asked you to go to putt-putt. That is *a date*. This deserves more attention...

I would . . . I would . . . I don't even know what I would do.

No way am I going to go on dates with boys. That's too much drama and intrigue, even for me.

Danny had his lemonade stand up today, so I took the twins by. He had one friend who was kind of being jerky, but Danny was pretty nice.

"So how much money are you making with all these views?" Danny asked.

"It's not about the money," I said.

"It doesn't have to be about the money. But it also doesn't hurt to make money anyway," he said.

"If I tip you an extra dollar, will you stop trying to put dollar signs on my dream?"

He shrugged. "Starving artist, huh? Okay. I got it."

Then Flynn knocked over a pitcher of lemonade. I gave Danny three bucks even though he said it was fine. I wanted to make some joke about it, or talk more, but his friend was there and . . . I don't know.

Then his friend left and I was walking away with the twins. Danny called me back.

"Piper. If you ever want to . . . come up with business ideas. Marketing ideas. Whatever. I think it'd be cool." He smiled, all straight teeth. "And I wouldn't charge you."

I think that was a compliment. I took it as one.

"All right. Because I have some ideas on how you run this stand," I said.

He raised his eyebrows. Both of them. Very few people can only raise one.

"Let's schedule a time next week." I took the twins' hands. "Later, Danny."

"Bye, Piper."

"How come he didn't call you Pepper like he used to?" Spencer asked.

Ay, caramba! I don't know.

Oh! And! Miss del Rosario gave me a present. A copy of *Anne of Green Gables*. She even wrapped it in sparkly paper and everything. She said it was her favorite book when she was a kid.

It is old and hard and almost in a whole other old-timey language. But she says there is Drama! Intrigue! Scandal!

So maybe someday I'll check it out. After I finish the Gallagher Girls series.

Maybe.

~P

Grateful: Future business meetings, lemonade, books that are about things I actually like, Miss Nikki, district video director!

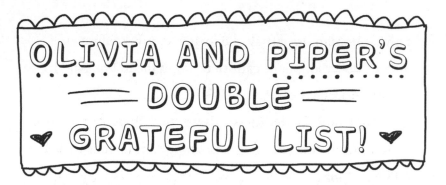

OLIVIA AND PIPER'S === DOUBLE === ♥ GRATEFUL LIST! ♥

Hear ye! Hear ye! This is the second installment of the first annual blessing of this notebook! We ask all pelicans flying overhead to please choose another direction until we can get this final grateful list written down without getting any poop on it.

Doing a grateful list at our sacred spot by the ocean was a great idea. Even though the fog is creeping in like a scary movie, so let's get on with this, shall we?

Olivia—Snickerdoodles, maple donuts, seaweed chips, Mom's cornbread

Piper—Oh, I get it . . . this one's food-related. Mashed potatoes. Those rock.

Olivia—Miss del Rosario, for letting me finally enjoy Battle of the Books

Piper—Miss del Rosario not having to bring out Marni puppet due to our awesome intervention

Olivia—Jordan, for always believing in my spelling abilities and my desire for phone calls that end in the Robot. And Jackson, for reading the books.

Piper—Danny, for business advice. Or whatever that was. This needs further research. You know, for business's sake.

Olivia—Books

Piper—Books. (Can you believe I just wrote that?)

Olivia—You. And all the pages left in this notebook.

Piper—You. And all the pages left in this notebo—

Seagulls this time??
Seriously, we need
an umbrella or something.

Acknowledgments

Lindsey,

Writing this book with you has been such a blast. I wish I could do everything with you. It would make folding laundry so much easier.

Making a book takes a village . . . so I want to thank our amazing team at HarperCollins. Editorial hugs to Catherine Wallace, Kristen Pettit, and Jen Klonsky, you all are so wonderful! Literary hugs to my agent, Jill Corcoran. Family hugs to Jayson, Luke, Mom, Dad, Buddy, Martin, Matt, and Ralph. Supportive friend hugs to Cammi and Eve. And chocolate hugs to all you Reese's candy bars out there—you are all important to me.

But I leave the biggest hug of all to you, dear Lindsey. You've made me want to be a better writer, better friend, better person. Your humor is boundless and your energy is contagious. I hope EVERYONE gets a chance to write a book with you someday. You have time for that, right?

Finally, a huge thanks to our readers. YOU are the reason why we do this. And the reason we will keep doing this.

Thank you.

Robin

Dear Robin,

Well . . . huh. That was like the most beautiful acknowledgment letter ever. Can I just add some emojis with a finger pointing up? Also, can we add some doodles? Love me some doodles.

Yes, our team at Harper was fun. Big thanks also to Abby Denning for taking all our random notes sprinkled throughout and turning this into a work of art. (I can say that because I'm referencing your amazing design, and not our writing, which ain't too shabby either.) Also, thank you to Sarah Creech, Alison Klapthor, Jessica Berg, Allison Brown, Vanessa Nuttry, Kim VandeWater, Megan Barlog, Mitchell Thorpe, Jessica Gould, and Jessica White.

Thanks to my jewel of an agent, Sarah Davies. To librarian Traci Dill for answering my numerous Battle of the Books questions. Also to Crystal Perkins for giving us the bestest launch ever. Also to Fred and Carolyn, for being my Book Tour Parents.

James. I used to think the kind of boys I wrote about were unicorns. Thank you for helping me find the truth amid all that fiction. You are goodness, light, laughter, and love personified. I'll take you any way I can get you, pleats and all. To Logan, Talin, Miles, Emilia, Rylee, and MacKay. How lucky am I to have such a long list of kids? How lucky am I to have

you in my life? How lucky am I to be a mom? Answer: Very.
Very very very.

To Mom and Dad and the rest of the Taylor family: You
have never wavered in your support, just as no sane person
would ever waiver in their love for the Giants. To my darling friends who are like my family (except we picked each
other)—cheers to my tribe.

Robin, it's been a wild ride. Thanks for grabbing my hand
and taking me with you. Writing never felt like work with
you. I wish every writer could experience the kind of magic
we shared.

Thank you.

Lindsey

Read them all!